Stand Against the Rising Storm

Desperate Disguise Book 2

Tessa Cole

Gryphon's Gate Publishing

Stand Against the Rising Storm

Gryphon's Gate Publishing
550 King St. N.
PO Box 42088 Conestoga
Waterloo, ON
N2L 6K5

Print ISBN: 978-1-990587-63-4

Reader Considerations

On top of my usual action scenes, spicy scenes, and profanity, this book contains an attempted sexual assault.

The moment takes place in the middle of chapter 34 and is brief.

A Quick Recap

My life changed forever when I took my brother Sawyer's place as a sacrifice to the Black Guard.

I couldn't let him go, not when I knew it was our cruel stepfather's way of getting rid of him, and certainly not after my premonition showed him dead in front of the Shadow Gate.

So when the boyishly handsome Lord Quill of the Black Guard delivered the summons, I seized my chance. I pressed my blood to the binding medallion instead of letting Sawyer do it, forever tying myself to the Black Tower.

But surviving as the only woman in the Guard while pretending to be a man was the least of my worries. My first night, I foolishly went through the fae ring after dark and was attacked by shadow hounds.

Only Lord Commander Rider's and Guardsman Grefin's intervention saved my life.

Then, after getting an eyeful of a naked Lord Talon, the Captain of the Gold Tower, I went to sleep and dreamed I was in a strange fae garden.

I appeared as a fae woman with long red hair and marks on my skin, and there, a mysterious man gave me pleasure beyond anything I'd experienced before.

Except it hadn't been a dream.

I'd really manifested my spirit into the fae's magical Garden as a fae woman.

But I didn't have time to worry about it. All of the guardsmen hated me. They saw me as a weak, entitled nobleman and were determined to put me in my place.

It had only been my first full day as a Guardsman and I was exhausted, sore, and confused. I couldn't stop thinking about how stunning Talon looked naked, and I couldn't stop looking at him, beautiful Lord Quill, and even gruff Lord Rider.

I yearned all day for another encounter with my Fantasy Man, even though I knew it was a terrible idea and the chances of me manifesting again in the fae's Garden were slim.

Then, just when I thought things couldn't get more complicated, I had another vision.

Now I was the one who was dead in front of the Shadow Gate.

CHAPTER 1
Sage

THE IMAGE OF MY BROKEN, bleeding body surrounded by swirling mist whirled around and around in my mind. Someone was going to kill me. Except I didn't know who or how or when or even where exactly.

All I really knew was that I was still in the Gray, still a Guardsman, and that they still thought I was a boy. Did they even know who I was supposed to be or had the attack been random? Had I just been at the wrong place at the wrong time? And who would attack a Guardsman in the Gray? I'd thought only Guardsmen and shadow monsters were in the Grey.

The vision had happened so fast, I hadn't gotten a good look at my surroundings. I had no idea where it was going to happen, only that the towering ominous Shadow Gate had been standing in the distance. But the Gate was so tall I didn't doubt it could be seen for miles around the Black Tower. I also had no idea who to watch out for, only that there'd been two of them.

The fear and cold within me deepened, sinking into my bones and making my hands shake.

I needed more information. With the vision of Sawyer's death, I'd had a sense of urgency, the knowledge that what I'd seen would happen soon. I had no idea when this new vision would come to pass. Vision—

Oh, Great Father! I was truly seeing things now. Twice in as many days and it had just come over me, stronger than the premonitions I used to have.

And both times I'd nearly collapsed. I probably would have fallen to my knees the first time if Lord Quill hadn't steadied me, which meant these visions were going to be harder to hide than my premonitions.

Before, I used to just blank out for a moment and look — according to Sawyer — like I was daydreaming. Falling to my knees was going to draw a lot more attention and I couldn't afford anymore attention. I had to figure out how to make them go away so I didn't expose myself—

No. Not the point.

The first thing I needed to do was to make sure what I'd seen didn't come to pass.

If I wasn't a Guardsman, the vision wouldn't come

true. Which meant I needed to reveal myself and beg for mercy from Lord Rider and the King of Erellod for lying. But I couldn't tell the truth until Sawyer was safely out of the Five Great Kingdoms and that would take at least a month, more if he had to sell his horse or ran into trouble.

Did I have that kind of time?

I squeezed my eyes shut, trying to remember what I'd seen, or hell, make the vision happen again. But the dizzying darkness and mist didn't sweep around me and the image of my broken body didn't reappear.

Of course, I hadn't been able to make my premonitions in the past happen, either, no matter how hard I'd tried. And I'd tried hard when Father had gone missing while hunting brigands and when Mother had fallen ill.

I'd been unable to sense where he'd gone or how to help her and had been just as helpless as everyone else in the end. The only *advantage* I'd had was the torture of knowing something bad was going to happen. At least with the visions, I had a clearer idea of what.

But it was foolish to think I could make these visions happen when I wanted them. I should be happy that I'd been warned about my impending death especially since I'd already been warned twice about Sawyer's yesterday.

Except, if I couldn't foresee when my latest vision

would happen did that mean I had to choose between my life or Sawyer's?

If it came to that, I'd choose Sawyer's. I'd do anything for him. I'd taken on the spell meant for him that bound a Guardsman to the Black Tower knowing the odds of him finding a way to break the spell and free me were slim.

I'd also known taking the spell meant if I left the Grey where the Black Tower stood and didn't return, the magic would kill me.

There were only a few ways for me to leave and none of them were good. If I revealed I was a girl, I'd be punished. And given Lord Rider's temper, the punishment would probably be severe before I was tossed back to Edred who might forego trying to sell me into marriage to just take his frustration out on me. And if I confessed too soon, they'd hunt Sawyer down and bind him to the Tower, making all the risks I'd already taken to save him pointless.

Hell, for all I knew Sawyer was still going to die in the Gray.

I thought I hadn't been able to change the outcome of my premonitions because I hadn't known what was going to happen, but there was still no guarantee that I'd be able to change it even though I could see what was coming.

But then what would be the point of seeing into the future?

My hands still trembling, I grabbed the edge of the basin secured to its stand and the wall in my small room and used it to steady myself as I stood.

There had to be a third option where neither of us died.

Dying meant our step-father, Edred, would win. He'd already manipulated the lottery and had Sawyer's name drawn, ensuring Sawyer would never succeed him as Marquis of Herstind March even though Sawyer was his heir and not yet sixteen.

I had no doubt that Edred had hoped the Gray would kill Sawyer. My brother's lungs were weak and while he might have survived the first day of Black Guard training, I knew — because I'd seen it — that he wouldn't have survived for many more.

So if I didn't know when the attack would come and I couldn't reveal myself for at least a month, then I had to make sure I was prepared.

I had to become the best fighter I could possibly be in as short a time as possible.

It wouldn't guarantee that I'd changed the future since I'd still be wearing the Black Guard's uniform, but it was better than revealing my secret and having Sawyer bound to the Tower.

At least now I knew the fight of my life was coming and I could prepare for it.

I finished washing off the day's grime as best as I could with just a small cloth, a bar of soap, and a basin of water that thankfully I could drain and refill as many times as I desired — thank you fae magic! Then I rewrapped the strips of cloth around my breasts, determined to ignore my achy sore muscles from a day of near-constant physical exertion and the pain from the dark purple bruise staining my chest and along my left side.

I'd slept naked my first night in the Tower because I'd had to wash my clothes and been in shock over escaping Edred then arriving in the Gray and being attacked by shadow monsters. Tonight, and for the rest of my time here, I wasn't going to be so foolish. I didn't have a lock on my door, and I still didn't know if those higher up the ranks liked to barge in on the sacrifices — pardon me, *novices*, as they insisted on calling us.

I pulled my shirt and pants back on then finally collapsed on my bed. Tomorrow was going to be another day of dirty looks and hissed remarks and mucking out the stables, not to mention whatever the Lord Commander of the Black Guard was going to throw at me.

So far he hadn't taken his temper out on me like Edred used to, but I didn't trust that he wouldn't. I'd made a serious mistake endangering Guardsmen's lives by using the fae ring after dark, and he and the rest of the Guard were angry about that.

But I'd take whatever they gave me. I had to. For Sawyer.

Exhaustion pulled at me and I let it drag me into darkness. I didn't think things would look better in the morning. In fact I was sure my body was going to hurt more when I woke, but at least I'd be rested.

The thought flittered through my mind, a spark dancing on a breeze, dimming then flaring, dimming then—

I gasped and jerked upright.

I'd thought of something... except I couldn't remember what. It had been there, at the edge of my thoughts. Something important, something—

My thoughts stuttered as my vision cleared.

Somehow I was in the fae's Garden again.

It was the same as last night. I sat on a patch of soft grass at the edge of a pool bathed in gentle moonlight. Long hair that I shouldn't have had because I'd cut it short like Sawyer's tickled my back and bare arms, and I wore the same soft, gauze and lace dress as before. It was cut low, revealing what little cleavage I had along with the strange red spots that encircled my neck and trailed down between my breasts.

I leaned forward and glanced at my reflection in the pool. Once again my hair was a vibrant red, darker and richer than my normal color, my eyes were a bright emerald, and my ears were pointed as if I were actually fae.

I brushed tentative fingers over my ear tips.

They felt real.

It didn't make sense. I wasn't fae. I didn't know how I could look fae when I manifested in the Garden or how I even manifested in the first place.

When I'd asked about it, Kit and Payne, the two fae Guardsmen who were on speaking terms with me, had been adamant that only fae could enter the Garden — spiritually or physically — and that there was magic that prevented humans from entering it.

I'd figured ending up in the Garden last night had been an accident, a mix of my strange fae-touched ability to sense the future combined with the fae magic binding me to the Tower — although don't ask me how that could have possibly helped me.

I hadn't thought I'd ever be here again.

And if I was here again, would I run into the Lord Commander or Talon or Lord Quill? What about the mystery man who I'd thought had been a fantasy who I'd let kiss and touch me in the most intimate way?

Heat burned my cheeks, half in embarrassment and half in desire. My body still throbbed with need from Talon using his magic on me in an attempt to force me to show him my bruise and prove I wasn't more hurt than I claimed to be, and that throbbing flared hot and needy between my thighs at the idea that Fantasy Man might be in the Garden right now.

Movement reflected in the pool caught my attention and I realized someone was sitting on the bench on the other side of the pool.

The last time I'd been here, three fae had practically pounced on me and then I'd been swarmed by dozens of men, which had been overwhelming, intimidating, and confusing.

And while I'd gotten the impression from Lord Rider that I could have told them to go away, everything I'd been taught said that a woman needed to be demure and comply with a man's wishes. My purpose was to obey and please my husband. Nothing more.

Which made me furious. Not all husbands deserved to be obeyed or pleased. That and I could be so much more than just my ability to please a man. My identity was mine, not my association to my father, step-father, brother, or husband.

Except I didn't know if I'd be able to fully resist a lifetime of discipline, not when it was just for myself. If Sawyer was with me and in danger, I'd have shouted and fought and not cared how disobedient I was. But just me... it was easier — and often less painful — to bow my head, say what they wanted me to say, then try to slip away.

I raised my eyes to the man on the bench and fell into Lord Rider's silver gaze for a heart-stopping moment. A hunger burned inside those silver orbs, a ferocity that I hadn't noticed before that stole my breath and made Talon's magic inside me burn hotter.

The spots around my neck and trailing between my breasts grew warm and pulsed in time with my suddenly pounding heart, and a tight heat swelled in my chest. Then he blinked and the hunger vanished and I was released from his gaze.

"I didn't think you'd return," he said, his voice gruff.

CHAPTER 2
Sage

"I DIDN'T THINK I'd return, either," I replied.

A warm breeze sighed through the grass, rippling the water between us and teasing a lock of hair at his temple.

Lord Rider wasn't as beautiful as Talon or Lord Quill, but he was still ruggedly handsome, and unlike me, who'd transformed into a fae with long hair and a red dress, he looked like he had at the Black Tower.

He wore his black clothes and armor and his weapons — or at least half of his weapons since he only had three or four daggers on him here in the Garden. His shoulder-length black hair with its silver streak was half pulled back in a topknot and half loose, and he still had those three thin silver scars slicing over the bridge of his nose and across his left cheek. And while he might have left the Gray before nightfall and been in the Garden in person, I suspected he'd manifested his spirit into the Garden like I had, which meant what I was looking at now was how his spirit actually appeared.

His eyes searched mine as if he was looking for something but I couldn't figure out what. "You look less stunned this time."

"You only think that because you're sitting over there and it's dark out."

I straightened, sending a whisper of pain thrumming through me. Except it was a ghost of what it had been moments ago in my room in the Black Tower, and I didn't know if that was because this wasn't really my body or because of something else.

The breeze sighed again, carrying with it deep, masculine laughter, drawing my attention to the courtyard behind Lord Rider. Inside, beyond the large statues of beautiful fae women and the green gauzy curtains, were a whole bunch of men far too eager for my attention.

Lord Rider glanced behind him, following my gaze up the path to the courtyard then turned back to me. "I'll stay until you get your bearings."

"Why would you do that?"

"My sister," he replied.

Right. He'd said last night that she'd been stunned the first time she'd manifested and he understood how disorienting it could be. Of course, then Talon had shown up, snapped at me, given Lord Rider a hard time about being with a woman, and then Lord Rider had made it clear he didn't want anything to do with me.

"You sure you want to be seen with me?"

The laugh came again and two beautiful fae men stepped out of the courtyard onto the path. Their gazes jumped to me as if I were a magnet, compelling them to look at me, and their expressions brightened with hope and desire. Lord Rider shifted on the bench, glared at them, and they hurried away without approaching me.

"You sure you want me to leave?" he replied.

He had a point. I wasn't ready to deal with the other men and their hungry need for me.

A shiver rushed over me. Well, I was certainly interested in one man's hungry need for me: my fantasy man. Except now that I knew this wasn't a dream, I was confused as hell as to why Fantasy Man's desire hadn't scared me like the other men's desire.

It had felt similar even though I'd never looked in his eyes and actually seen it. But somehow it had been different, like he was supposed to desire me like that.

I stood and Lord Rider — no, here he was just Rider — moved to the edge of the stone bench, offering me as much space on the small seat as possible which wasn't much given how big and bulky he was.

But that only reminded me that he was the gruff Lord Commander of the Black Guard who didn't like me. Was his change in behavior toward me because I was a woman here and he was kind to women?

No, it was probably because in the Gray he thought I was an idiot and didn't have the patience for idiots regardless of their gender and here he'd yet to form an opinion on me.

"I don't know how much you remember from last night," he said as I sat. "I'm Rider."

My shoulder accidentally brushed his as I settled and more need thrummed through me, making me tremble.

Swell.

Thanks to Talon, I was desiring not just Fantasy Man, but the Lord Commander as well and that just had trouble written all over it.

"Sage," I replied, my voice breathy. "Are you meeting the same men tonight?"

"You mean is Talon going to show up and be an asshole?" Rider growled. "No. We've already met this evening. He's off fucking someone. Or he better be."

I raised my eyebrows at that.

"Fuck, sorry," he said, his gaze turning apologetic then slipping away from me as if he were embarrassed to maintain eye contact. "Guess that was crude. I'm not used to female company."

He worked entirely with men and had been doing

it long enough to become the Lord Commander of the Black Guard. 'Not used to female company' was an understatement.

I snorted a quick laugh then realized how rude that was and tensed, ready to be admonished for my unfeminine behavior.

"My sister doesn't count," he added, as if he hadn't noticed my unladylike snort and needed to offer more of an explanation. "I'm a Guardsman at the Black Tower. I don't have contact with a lot of women."

Just a Guardsman. Not the Lord Commander. This was becoming a really weird conversation. Rider was confident and gruff at the Tower. Here he was almost awkward, as if he were afraid or didn't know how to be in a woman's company. If I hadn't known without a doubt this was real, I'd have said this was my weirdest dream yet.

"You know your sister might be upset that she doesn't count as a woman."

"Nope. She knows I'm a disaster around women." He huffed his own quick laugh. "Pretty sure I've said more to you in this conversation than I have to any woman since..." His expression darkened. "Why didn't you think you'd be returning?"

"I—" *Well that was a sudden change of conversation.* "I just didn't."

I shrugged and left it at that since I couldn't say I

hadn't thought I'd return because I was really a human and shouldn't have been here in the first place.

"Is your sister here?" I asked, making my own sharp turn in our conversation.

"She's with her mates. She only has a few more days left in her conception cycle and..." His expression grew even darker.

That look had flickered across his face last night as well when she'd pressed her hands to her belly and her eyes had filled with the obvious hope that she'd become pregnant.

"You're worried about her."

"She wants a child so much, but she's been trying for a long time with no success. One of these cycles she's going to realize it isn't possible and it's going to break her heart," he said, his voice gruff.

"That's terrible." I didn't know what else to say to that. No one should have to deal with the pain of realizing they'd never have their heart's desire.

Except that thought made me wonder what my heart's desire was and my thoughts instantly jumped to Fantasy Man. I wanted to see him again and have him bring me pleasure again and again.

And while yes, I desperately wanted that, I also wanted to be free, to make my own choices, and not have to obey someone else's whims.

"Her mates will get her through it." He shrugged and glanced back in the direction Lark had gone last night. The direction that I now knew led to the maze-like grove with all the bedrooms and nooks and soft, magical glowing flowers, and where Fantasy Man had made me—

My breath picked up, and that need Talon had awakened flared stronger, hot and achy within me.

"They're good men. But..." he said.

"But you're her brother and you'd do anything to protect her," I finished for him, trying to focus on the conversation and not my body's growing desires.

Except Rider's silver gaze slid back to me and captured my soul, adding to the heat in my marks and around my heart and between my thighs. Then laugher in the courtyard behind us drew his attention away, and I was released once again.

"I'd do anything for her," he replied.

"I know how you feel. I have a brother I'd do anything for." That I was already doing *everything* for and was facing certain death if I didn't figure out how to defend myself or stop whatever was coming.

Except— *oh crap.* I'd taken on Sawyer's binding spell. Rider had looked at my forearm where the spell had sank into me when I'd first arrived and I could only assume he'd been able to tell I'd been enspelled. Could he see it now?

No, that was silly. I didn't know him very well, but he struck me as an observant man, which meant he would have noticed the binding spell by now.

"I take it your brother isn't of age," Rider said, making me frown in confusion. "If he was, even if you'd manifested by accident last night, he would have been here to show you the Garden tonight. Unless you haven't told your family you're manifesting."

"My brother had to leave home and I have no other family," I said, the truth slipping from my tongue.

"So there's no one here for you?" Now it was Rider's turn to frown. "How do you not have any other family? Where's your mother and her mates and their families."

"I—" Because they were dead. And even though Edred was technically now the man in charge of my life, he didn't count as family.

Except from Rider's response, it sounded like even if my mother and father had died there'd be other family members to take care of me. Lark had four mates. Did all fae woman have multiple mates? And if that was the case, all those men likely had brothers and sisters and mothers and multiple fathers as well. With that many people connected to each other, I doubted fae children were ever abandoned like human children.

"Why don't you show me the Garden." It was another obvious change in subject and I prayed Rider wouldn't push me for details.

I didn't know if coming to the Garden a second time was another accident or not, but if it wasn't and I was going to keep showing up here every time I fell asleep, I couldn't risk anyone finding out I wasn't who I seemed to be. I didn't know if that would affect what happened at the Black Tower or not, but it was a chance I didn't want to take.

That, and I didn't want to push Rider away. Here I could actually talk to him, be near him, stare at him as much as I wanted, something I couldn't do in the Gray despite the aching need that compelled me to stare every time he or Talon or Lord Quill were near.

Maybe if I got my fill of looking at him here, I'd be able to stop looking at him when I was supposed to be Sawyer.

Except Rider jerked to his feet as if I'd burned him, his expression suddenly hard. "No. I— I've forgotten myself. Ask someone else."

CHAPTER 3
Sage

RIDER'S FORM SHIMMERED, turned see-through, then dissolved like a puff of smoke in a gentle breeze, melting away into nothing.

I stared at where he'd been, stunned by his reaction. It was as if I'd asked him to do something horrible and not just show me the Garden, or as if he were angry at me. Except I had no idea what I'd said wrong.

Of course maybe asking him to show me the Garden had been inappropriate. He'd tried to get Lark to show me the first time. Perhaps men weren't supposed to show women the Garden. But that didn't make sense. Dozens of men had offered to show me all manner of things last night when I'd been swarmed in the courtyard.

Speaking of the courtyard...

More laughter yanked me from my thoughts. If I

didn't want a repeat of last night, I needed to find some place more private and then I needed to figure out how Rider had disappeared like that. I assumed he'd stopped his spirit from manifesting and had returned to his body, which was something I needed to do before those hungry men overwhelmed me again.

Except my heated need hadn't chilled when Rider had abruptly vanished and I really didn't want to wake in the Black Tower sore from yesterday's labor, hurting from Edred's beating, *and* aching with unfulfilled desire.

Masculine voices said something, not quite loud enough for me to tell what they were saying, and two men pushed aside the gauzy green curtain separating the courtyard from the rest of the garden and stepped onto the path. Their attention instantly leaped to me, as if like the others they'd instinctually known where I was, and even in the dim moonlight I could see the hunger in their eyes.

Without a doubt, I could have almost every man here, more than one at the same time just like Lark if I was brave enough to ask for that, but their looks continued to make me nervous despite my desire.

Waking up disappointed was probably the safest decision. I could touch myself and relieve the pressure and carry on with my day. I certainly didn't want to find myself in a situation where I couldn't get away.

I jerked my attention away from them, hoping

they'd get the point, and hurried down a path leading away from the courtyard. Before I realized where I was going, I was passing the pools, the soft moans of fae having sex making my need burn hotter, and hurrying through the impossible stone and living-tree arch into the winding passages of the magical grove.

Here the light grew dimmer, softer, the path illuminated not by bright fae lanterns but by moonlight and gently glowing white and pink flowers that grew from vines entwined around arches and fences and screens.

The magical warmth and peace of the place seeped into my skin, radiating through my body all the way to my fingers and toes and surged around my heart, even as my need tightened and swelled.

I wasn't going to be able to wait to figure out how to stop manifesting. I needed to relieve the pressure building inside me in order to concentrate on figuring that, or anything, out.

I reached the two-way split in the path that was actually a three-way split and took the almost hidden, darker, narrower path back to the nook where I'd first watched Lark and her mates have sex and then had let Fantasy Man put his mouth on me.

The nook was even more dimly lit than before, the light from the flowers barely visible and no light shone through the silver and vine screen offering a glimpse into the bedroom beyond which was empty.

But I didn't need to watch Lark having sex to get

excited. I was already on the verge, my moisture dampening my thighs, my body thrumming, aching for release.

I stepped from the stone path onto the soft mossy ground and headed to the wide cushioned bench. It sat in the center of the nook, wide enough for two people to lie close together, with its gently sloped arms that offered a perfect, private place to lie back and stare at the stars... or in my case, touch myself.

The thought made heat sweep over my cheeks and down my neck. I'd never touched myself before, not with the express purpose of making myself come. It was a wonton act inappropriate for a noblewoman. Proper women didn't touch themselves.

My gaze strayed back to the dark bedroom. Proper women didn't enjoy watching other people have sex.

And none of that mattered. If I didn't do something, I was going to burst. I didn't know what had come over me, but the heat in my body and the heat in the strange spots around my neck and down my chest, was too much.

I stretched out on the bench, leaning against the arm that faced the nook's only entrance not wanting to be caught touching myself, and captured both my breasts in my hands. I wasn't at all sure what I was doing, but it felt good.

The memory of Lark's men kissing and licking and

touching her swept into my mind's eye and I ran my thumbs over my nipples over top of my dress.

I closed my eyes, and tried to imagine one of Lark's men above me. But they were taken and fantasizing about them felt wrong.

Then Talon's image popped into mind. He was breathtakingly beautiful, his face and body sculpted to perfection, his long hair pale with shimmering strands of silver, and his eyes... Oh Great Father his eyes! They were a mesmerizing swirl of pink and purple and blue and gold and could hold my soul captive for an eternity.

He was perfect. He might be mean to me in the Garden, but he was shockingly kind to me in the Gray and I'd seen him naked. All of him. It was easy to imagine his muscular body or his long, thick cock.

Rider had said he was in the Garden having sex with someone right now, but I hadn't gotten the impression he was in a relationship and I didn't have the same problems fantasizing about him as I did with Lark's men.

I slid my hands inside my plunging neckline and pushed the thin, gauzy fabric aside, exposing my breasts. I imagined Talon looking down at me, his desire darkening his stunning eyes, and then he'd teased my tightening nipples between his thumbs and fingers.

I squirmed, rolling my nipples as I imagined Talon

would, my breath catching at the delicious pinch and the sensual fantasy. He'd suck one into his mouth with another soft pinch and roughly palm the other one.

My need twisted tighter and I played with my breasts, teasing myself like I fantasized Talon would, making me gasp and squirm with a desire that was quickly growing into an inferno. Then he'd slide a hand down my body, inch up my dress, and torment me in the most amazing way with his fingers.

I tugged up my dress, letting my legs fall open, and trailed my fingers up my inner thigh, swirling closer and closer to my wet slit.

But he wouldn't go there straight away. He'd keep up the teasing, brushing a finger in my wetness, sending a whisper of a touch against my sensitive nub.

I skimmed that nub, sending sensation snapping through me and making my breath hitch before I released it on a soft, aching moan.

Oh, yes. I just wished it really was Talon, or Fantasy Man—

My thoughts stuttered and the image of Talon melted into Lord Quill, with his shy boyish smile, his golden-blond hair catching the sunlight as if it were really gold, and his thoughtful emerald eyes.

I skimmed my finger across my nub again, sending another shudder of sensation rushing through me.

My breath picked up even as the image in my mind shifted to Rider, which should have killed the mood but didn't. He'd been awkward around me, but I had a feeling he'd be like Lark's mate, Blaze, ferocious and consuming in his lovemaking. Rider wouldn't just skim my nub, he'd push his fingers inside me, he'd work me hard, overwhelming me, possessing me, bringing me to the heights of pleasure all while keeping me safe.

I groaned as I slid a finger inside me then slowly slid it out. Rider wouldn't be slow, but going slow felt so good.

My muscles trembled and my body burned with the delicious fire threatening to consume me.

I grasped my breast tighter and pushed my finger back in, turning the man in my mind's eye back to Talon. He'd go slow. He'd draw it out, work me to the edge, building up both me and Rider then let Rider take over.

Something snapped and I froze, my breath stalling and my eyes flying open and jumping to the nook's entrance. A man stood in the narrow archway, the light from the flowers not quite reaching his face.

The heat of embarrassment seared my cheeks, as I stared at him with a finger buried inside me and one hand clutching my breasts.

"Please," the man said, his voice husky with desire and oh-so-familiar. Fantasy Man. "Don't stop on my account."

"I'd rather you took over," I replied, my voice just as husky, my words shocking me.

CHAPTER 4
Sage

"If you're serious about that," Fantasy Man purred, sending a delicious shiver racing through me, "you'll remove your dress and let me see you."

"I'm pretty sure you're already seeing a lot of me." I dropped my gaze down my body to where my legs were spread and slowly slid my finger out of myself, still shocked by my boldness.

Anyone else and I would have snapped my legs closed and covered myself, but there was something about Fantasy Man that made me feel confident and sexy… or maybe it was something about this Garden or this magical grove that dropped my inhibitions.

"Is that a no?" he asked, his tone sensual and deep, making my core throb.

"No," I breathed as I reached for the ties at my side securing my dress then realized that my answer was unclear. "I mean, it's a yes." I fumbled with the ties. Saying yes was also unclear. "I mean—"

"Stand up, turn around, and I'll help," he said with a chuckle.

I stood and turned my back to him, listening for his footsteps drawing close, but I didn't hear anything. One moment I was in the middle of the nook by myself, the next I could feel the heat from his body against my back. Then he brushed my hair aside and pressed his lips against the sensitive spot just behind my ear.

A shiver rushed through me and the desire I'd built up by myself twisted sharp and needy.

"I see you like to torture yourself as well," he murmured against my skin, reminding me that Lark's mate, Blaze, liked to build up his desire until he couldn't stand it any longer and he succumbed to his passion.

"Not to the same extent as Blaze," I replied, my voice still breathy. "But I can see the appeal." If I hadn't wanted the tease, I wouldn't have drawn out touching myself. I would have just released the sexual pressure building inside me and moved on. But then I might not have been here for Fantasy Man to find me.

His hands nudged mine away from my laces. "How much more can you take?"

He loosened the laces then slowly slid my dress from my shoulders, his fingers skimming my skin. My pulse stuttered, and he knelt behind me, pushing the dress past my hips to pool around my feet, then teased his lips against the back of my thigh.

"Not much more," I breathed. I was already on the edge, aching from when I'd touched myself... hell, from before I'd touched myself.

"Are you sure?" He slid his hands up the insides of my thighs, his touch so much more than my fantasy. It shot hot, needy sensation to my core, and tightened a desire that I'd thought had already been twisted to its limit.

"I'm not sure you're ready for me," he said, his breath feathering against my thighs.

"I'm ready," I gasped, then his fingers dipped into my wetness, just a whisper of a touch, and my breath vanished completely. A low, throaty moan escaped my lips and my legs trembled, threatening to give out.

"Ah, you're right," he chuckled. "But still—"

He stood and swept his arm around my waist, pulling me back against his chest and supporting me, while his other hand pushed past my curls and returned to my slit. His fingers teased me, sliding my slickness against my sensitive nub, making my muscles tighten and tremble on the edge of that incredible sensation he'd given me last night, but always stopping before I crashed over.

He tormented me until I was writhing in his grasp, my breath fast, moans and mewling gasps escaping my lips, and my legs were unable to hold me up. Then he turned me to the bench and urged me to kneel on it, facing away from him.

I trembled in anticipation, waiting for him to take me, aching for him to finish what we'd started. If this was what sex was like, then my first time with Royston didn't count at all. It had been quick and unsatisfying, and I'd felt like I'd only been there to please him. Not that Royston had intended it to be that way. He had tried to please me, but we'd both been young and inexperienced, and I doubted he'd known that sex could be something like this.

Fantasy Man drew close behind me, the heat from his body blazing against my bare skin. I tried to look back at him, see his expression, but the light was too low and his jaw-length hair hung loose and shadowed his face.

"Goddess, you're so beautiful." He slid his hands inside my thighs, urging me to open a little wider for him, sending jolts of lightning snapping across my skin where he touched me.

The heat around my heart and from my spots blazed stronger and I pushed my rear back, desperate to be filled, to release the pressure inside me that he'd only increased with his teasing. His erection brushed the inside of my thigh, sending a shuddering whisper of a climax racing through me, making me moan.

He groaned in response and then his tip pressed against my entrance.

I tensed, and for a moment I was afraid that despite my body's aching need for him to be inside me, this sex would be as uncomfortable as the sex I'd had with Royston.

But he gripped my hips, holding me steady, and carefully pushed inside me with no pain, only an incredible slick pressure as he filled me.

He moved slowly, giving my body time to adjust to him, and both of us were panting with need by the time he'd fully sheathed himself inside me. More jolts snapped up and down my spine, and now he trembled just like me.

"Oh, fuck." His grip on my hips tightened, his fingers digging into my flesh, and he sucked in sharp desperate breaths.

The tremor of a climax, that incredible sensation he'd shown me last night, tightened my muscles and his groan deepened.

"Oh, fuck fuck fuck," he hissed then he slowly withdrew and pushed back in a little faster and harder, sending another, stronger tremor shuddering through me

Oh, fuck indeed. A hint of stars fluttered behind my lids and I teetered on that incredible edge. So close. Please. I needed the release so much it hurt.

He thrust again and again, quickly building up

speed, harder and faster as if he knew I wasn't going to last, that my release was going to come crashing down at any moment.

The heat and pressure inside me swirled, faster and faster. I spun tight, desperate. *Oh shadows. Shadows!*

Then an explosion of pleasure roared through me, ripping a cry from my lips as I crashed over the edge. Power and light flooded me, spinning me around and around and around, and I was enveloped in incredible, glorious heat.

Fantasy Man kept thrusting, hard and fast, chasing his own release, and quickly followed. He tensed and let out a low, masculine moan that sent another shudder of sensation swelling through me, adding to the rush already overwhelming me.

That was—

That was—

Oh, Great Father! That was—

I didn't know how to put it into words and I couldn't make my mind work. It was amazing and perfect. I felt sexy and powerful and boneless and spent.

CHAPTER 5
Sage

I SAGGED FORWARD and pressed my cheek against the soft seat cushion, gasping for breath. I didn't care that my butt was in the air or that Fantasy Man was still buried inside me. In fact, I loved that he was still there, his cock pulsing with his heartbeat, the heat from his body somehow still blazing against my bare skin even though my insides had been flooded with warmth. His touch still sent whispers of lightning tickling through my skin and his hot breath washed warm and sensual over my back.

"And you managed to stay this time." He slid himself out of me and before I could figure out what I was supposed to do with a stranger who'd just brought me the most incredible pleasure of my life, he wrapped his arms around me, laid back against the bench's arm, and held me against his chest.

"I managed to stay?" He was still dressed, but his jerkin was made of a soft dark material, so I rested my cheek over his heart, listening to it race, still pounding from what we'd done, and melted into his embrace.

It should have been strange letting him hold me. It should have been really strange letting him touch and enter me. I still had no idea what his name was or even what he looked like. But when I went to raise my head, he stroked his fingers through my hair, urging me to stay resting against him.

"Just stay like this," he murmured, a wistful, yearning sadness edging his tone. "Please. Just for a moment."

There was something so broken, so resigned about his tone, as if he had a fate he didn't want but had accepted it.

It made my heart hitch and I relaxed against his touch, willing to give him this comfort even though I didn't know what I was comforting him from. I didn't feel uncomfortable with him despite knowing nothing about him. In fact, I felt safe, safer than I'd ever felt before, and staying wrapped in his arms, drifting in this moment of peace, my worries momentarily forgotten, was a comfort for me, too.

It didn't make sense, especially since I knew this wasn't a dream, but I supposed if he'd wanted to hurt me, he'd had plenty of opportunities to do so already.

"What did you mean by I managed to stay this time?" I asked, snuggling into his embrace.

"Last night you lost control of your spirit form when you came." His fingers continued to stroke gentle lines across my temple and through my hair, relaxing me even more. "You almost lost it tonight, but managed to hold on."

The image of Rider turning to smoke and vanishing popped into my mind's eye.

Fantasy Man had still been going when I'd come, so... "If I hadn't managed to stay, that would have left you..." I wasn't sure how to finish that sentence.

"A very unhappy man," he chuckled. "So I'm glad you stayed."

"Me too. And I'm glad you found me tonight." I hadn't necessarily been looking for him, but a part of me had really hoped to see him again this evening.

"Oh, I'm pretty sure you would have been just fine on your own," he replied.

"Fine, sure. But not great." I released a satisfied sigh, drawing another soft laugh. "Thank you. I didn't know sex could feel that way."

"If it doesn't, you're doing it wrong." He pressed his lips against the top of my head and tightened his grip around my waist as if he couldn't get me close enough. "You should probably go."

His grip belied his words, but still something in me fluttered in disappointment.

I didn't want this moment to end. I'd thought coming to the fae's Garden last night had been a mistake and even though I'd shown up tonight, it still could be a mistake.

One of these nights I might go to bed and not wake up in the Garden, and I didn't think I'd ever feel this good again. I certainly didn't know if I'd ever feel this safe or comfortable in a man's arms.

I hadn't even felt this way with Royston. Having sex with him had been a way to get back at Edred, not because we'd been in love, but because I wanted control over something, anything.

As a nobleman's daughter, Edred controlled my entire life and I'd been determined not to let him have control of my first sexual experience. Of course that quick encounter had been a huge disappointment compared to my second and third experiences.

I released another satisfied sigh and turned my attention to the patch of stars above me, visible through a large break in the leafy canopy that covered this magical grove.

"Do you have somewhere you have to be?" I asked.

His fingers in my hair stilled. "I don't."

"Then let's stay like this for a bit and look at the stars. They're beautiful tonight."

His fingers resumed their mesmerizing strokes, lulling my already relaxed body even more. "Not as beautiful as you."

"Oh, you don't know I'm beautiful," I replied. "I could be really ugly on the inside."

"But someone ugly on the inside wouldn't have pointed that out."

"Unless I'm trying to trick you into thinking I'm beautiful," I shot back, making him chuckle. Great Father I loved that sound. Rich and masculine and sensual. "I don't understand how this isn't a dream. I don't know you, don't know your name, don't even know what you look like, but I feel safe. I wish I didn't have to go back."

I didn't know if fae women had more freedom than human women, but it wouldn't matter if I could just stay like this with him forever.

Except what would happen to Sawyer if I didn't return? I had no idea what my body was doing while I was here in the Garden. If I stayed, I probably wouldn't wake up and then I'd be discovered and—

Crap. I had to get back. Giving in to this desire, this comfort, was a mistake. I'd almost forgotten my purpose and endangered my brother's life. I couldn't have Fantasy Man *and* Sawyer's safety. It was one or the other, and Sawyer's life was more important than my happiness.

Besides, I wasn't fae and I didn't want to see Fantasy Man's disappointment when he learned the truth.

"You were right," I said, my throat and chest tightening. I didn't want to leave him. It didn't make sense. I didn't know him, but my soul hurt thinking this could be the last time I saw him... and knowing it *should* be the last time I saw him. "I have to go."

"I know, Red. It's okay." He pressed his lips against the top of my head and I drifted away, my consciousness sinking into darkness and my soul tight with grief.

CHAPTER 6
Ash

I WOKE in my bed in the Black Tower, buried my face in my pillow, and screamed. I was an idiot. I was a Goddess damned idiot. And feeling that surge of power and peace rushing through me when I'd fully buried myself in Red's hot, tight sheath wasn't worth the pain of being reminded of what connecting with a woman felt like.

Goddess, I needed that connection like I needed to breathe and it shredded my soul knowing it would never be mine. *She* would never be mine.

What the hell was wrong with me? I'd been getting along just fine not remembering that I was missing a part of myself. I fucked humans when I needed a release and I'd been fine.

Fine!

Then I stumble across that stunning, shocking

redhead, who made the something inside me that needed a mate whisper, cajole, and taunt me, and I lost my fucking mind.

I shouldn't have teased her last night and I sure as hell shouldn't have stuck my cock in her tonight.

But her desire while watching Lark had been mesmerizing and tonight—

Oh Goddess, tonight!

I'd needed time to think about the three novices who the others had told me to keep an eye on to make sure they adjusted to their new, unwanted life, and didn't try to kill themselves. I'd also needed to think about the possible troublemakers I'd already identified. And while I could have done my thinking here in the Tower, I'd found myself wandering back to the nook where I'd first seen Red.

I hadn't thought I'd been going to the nook to look for her. I often sat in that nook to think because it was private, very few people knew about it, and the bedroom it looked into usually wasn't in use.

But then I saw her on the bench with her head tipped back in pleasure, her mating marks glowing red and pulsing with her desire, and the bodice of her dress pushed aside, exposing her gorgeous, small breasts. Her legs had been spread wide with her dress hiked up to her waist showing me everything, especially how turned on she was, and her finger had been sliding in and out of her slick entrance.

My whole essence had snapped to her and everything else had vanished: my worries over the novices and the trouble various humans and fae were up to in their realms, along with the soul-deep ache of knowing I'd never be mated.

She was stunning, and not just because she was physically beautiful. There was something else about her, something that stole my breath.

I huffed into my pillow.

She made me forget myself, forget that once she actually saw me, she'd be disgusted and never want to be with me again. Every woman who'd seen the real me had looked at the ugly, rough, red scars marring my right cheek with disgust.

And even though I had the magical ability to change my appearance everywhere else, I couldn't do it in the Garden. I couldn't even get my spirit form to look the way it had before the horrible night when I'd been burned. My bad decision and the death of that child had been scarred on my body *and* my soul, and because of that, I'd never fulfill my soul's need to have a mate.

And there was no way I'd be able to be with Red again, not without her seeing me.

It had actually shocked me that she hadn't fought me when she'd tried to look up at me and I'd stopped her. But she'd accepted my request to just lie together and had snuggled her perfect body against mine, making me hard all over again even though I'd just had an incredible release.

My soul sang for her, wanted her, begged that she'd fall in love with me and the Goddess would bind us together.

Fuck.

I punched my mattress and screamed into my pillow again.

Fuck fuck fuck. Shadow shit! Fuuuuuck!

No more. I needed to forget about her, do my fucking job, and when the novices got lieu time, get my ass to the pleasure house in Lehyrst and fuck myself into forgetting what Red felt like and sounded like and tasted like.

Fuck! It was a terrible plan.

But it was the only thing I could do. I had to forget about her and I sure as hell couldn't see her again. Not even a glimpse.

Except I couldn't tell Rider I didn't want to meet in the Garden anymore for our command meetings — that would bring up too many questions I didn't want to deal with. I'd just have to make sure I returned to my body the instant the meetings were done.

Red's mating marks were full and bright which meant her soul was on the hunt for her mates. Her sexual hunger was increased which was why she'd been so enthralled by Lark and her mates, and why I'd found her fingering herself in the nook.

Of course that didn't explain why she hadn't found some other man to satisfy her and had been doing it herself. The whole point of a woman's increased desires when her marks awakened was to find her best mates. She should be having sex with as many eligible men as possible to find those who were fated for her.

The idea of her having sex had my cock hardening and my balls tightening all over again.

I wanted to have her again and again. I wanted to watch her find her mates, see that glorious look of absolute bliss rush across her expression and listen to her moan and sigh and beg with pleasure. I wanted—

To Goddess-damned not think about her and sex!

And really, that hadn't been the point of my train of thought. The point was that she needed to make connections with as many men as possible to find her mates, and I could only pray that would happen quickly. Once she'd bound them to her, my soul would know there was no hope for me and I could forget about her.

And for now, I needed to get back to work.

Get. Back. To. Work.

The first bell rang, telling me it was time to get up and eat, and I struggled to shove the memory of Red as deep down inside me as I could. I had a smith, a farmer, and a boy to keep an eye on, and Talon was particularly worried about the boy.

Of course Talon's shadow wanted to fuck the boy

which was another problem, and Talon wasn't sure if he should continue the tentative friendship he was developing with Sawyer Herstind or keep his distance.

From what he and Quill told me, Talon's shadow's magic had enthralled the boy even while Talon was dressed and not trying to seduce him, something I hadn't seen happen for almost sixty years, and Talon was afraid the boy would be compelled to his bed against his will.

But, because everything with Talon was fucking complicated, he was afraid if he started keeping his distance from the boy, it would make Sawyer feel even more isolated than he already was, and with the boy pissing off most of the Guard, he had very few friends at the moment.

I got dressed and joined the stream of men heading into the great hall, remembering to look like I was seeing everything for the first time and not like I was ready to kill someone — like how I felt... because I let myself taste something I desperately wanted and knew I'd never have.

Goddess!

I ran my hands through my messy, short-cropped brown hair, and strained to concentrate. Thankfully my magic to change my appearance didn't require a lot of concentration to maintain. I could even hold it, keeping my identity a secret, while being tortured... not that I wanted to retest that anytime soon.

This time around — I'd forgotten how many times I'd disguised myself as a novice — I'd picked the persona of a soldier so I didn't have to look completely overwhelmed and I didn't have to work so hard to be a terrible fighter. The Guardsman's life was similar to that of any grunt in any army with the exception that Guardsmen were treated better than most grunts. We had our own room with a basin and pump, a bathhouse under the barracks, and a wide variety of fresh food regardless of the season in the human or fae realms thanks to a little fae magic.

The arrangement was to ensure the fae were happy, since we volunteered for the Guard, but it also had the added benefit of helping the humans. They weren't given a choice to join the Black Guard. Their names were drawn from a lottery, and they were torn away from whatever life they'd had and spent the rest of their short existence here.

I entered the great hall, joined the line leading into the kitchen, and scanned the long tables and benches filling the large space while I waited to get my food.

The great hall was the biggest room in the Black Tower, rising two stories high with large windows over the double doors at the front and along both walls. Right now very little light shone through the windows since it was just past dawn, and the room was lit by magical lanterns and two fires in the enormous hearths on either side of the room.

Hamelin, a novice who'd also been a soldier before his name was drawn in the human's lottery, sat with Durand, Bramwell, and Mikel. These were the four humans who had the most combat skill and experience and it made sense that they'd be drawn to each other.

Durand, Bramwell, and Mikel were all from families who trained potential Guardsmen. Mikel and Durand's families were situated in Addur, the capital of the kingdom of Erellod, while Bramwell's was in the capital of Irialas, a neighboring kingdom.

For a fee of course, these families sent their sons to the Gray in place of a nobleman's son — since only first born noblemen's sons were exempt from the lottery.

They were also the four most likely to give the other human novices a difficult time since the other novices were mostly farmers and merchants and had little to no fighting experience.

Everyone when they first arrived, including the novices who were fae, tried to find where they fit in the Guard. Fae usually fit in fine.

We were bigger, stronger, and faster than humans, and while most fae Guardsmen didn't have magic, a few of us did, making it easy for us to become the warriors we needed to be to defend the Gates of the Realms.

The humans however struggled. There were those

who were never going to be strong fighters and they usually got sentry duty on the Tower's wall and support positions with extra duties in the kitchen, infirmary, or with the quartermaster.

Those humans who could fight and fight well, knew they belonged right away and sometimes made a point of letting those who weren't as skilled know exactly how unskilled they were... something that was likely going to happen with this year's group of novices.

CHAPTER 7
Ash

I FOLLOWED the line of men into the kitchen, grabbed my breakfast, and stepped back into the hall on the other side. As expected, Hamelin and Bramwell waved me over to join them and I flashed them a smile I didn't feel.

"Hey, Ambrose," Hamelin called out as I approached. He was a big bulky man with a thick scar running down his cheek that twisted the right side of his mouth up in a perpetual sneer, belying his overall good nature. "What did you think of the bed? Sure beats a blanket on hard ground."

"How often were you sleeping on the ground?" I asked. There weren't a lot of military campaigns happening in the Great Five Kingdoms at the moment, so Hamelin should have spent most of his time in his army base's barracks.

He shrugged as I sat beside him. "My last two years I spent in the Minimien Borderlands in Irialas hunting chimeras."

Bramwell's eyes widened. He was from Irialas and looked like a typical Irialian with wavy blond hair cut just short enough that it didn't get in his blue-gray eyes that were the color of a stormy sea, and he knew just how difficult and pervasive the chimera infestation was. "You were in the Borderlands?"

"Yeah." A shadow slipped over Hamelin's expression and he dug into his bowl of porridge, his sudden change in demeanor making it clear he didn't want to talk about it. "What do you think we're doing this afternoon?"

"I heard they're testing us on how well we can fight from horseback today," Durand replied. He was the smallest of the four but only by half a head and while his build was also a little smaller and leaner than the others, it was similar to the one I'd picked for myself—and one that was actually quite close to my regular lean-muscled build.

Hamelin groaned. "Well that sucks. I can ride well enough not to fall off if the beast starts running, but that's about it."

Mikel rolled his eyes at him. He was the most handsome of the group with a muscular honed physique, brown eyes that were sharp with intelligence, and short brown hair. He was also a good fighter, knew it, and had no problem making sure everyone else knew it as well. He could probably win fights against half of the fae in the Guard already… if his overconfidence didn't get him in trouble.

"I doubt you'll be worse than the farmers," he said. "They don't even know how to swing a sword."

"Or shoot a bow," Bramwell added with a chuckle.

"I wonder how *the lord* will do?" Durand asked with a sneer.

"Probably pretty well," Hamelin said with a sigh. "Being a lord and all, he's probably been trained to fight from horseback. What I can't believe is how fast he is with a sword."

Which was true. The boy was damned fast, almost as fast as some of the fae, and knew that was his advantage in a fight.

"Yeah, but one hit and he's down," Durand huffed, "and we all know the Lord Commander didn't hit him that hard. We were all hit, several times."

"He's going to need to toughen up if he's going to be a Guardsman," Bramwell added.

Mikel leaned forward. "It's going to be up to us to do that. The Lord Commander stopped the fight the instant the runt dropped and did you see Talon? He hung back after training probably to check on him."

Durand nodded his agreement. "They're fae. They probably think he's still a child because he's so much smaller than them. But coddling won't help him become a man."

"I don't care if he becomes a man or not," Hamelin said. "If he can't hold his own in a fight, I don't want him at my back."

Which was probably how everyone in the Guard felt about Sawyer. Even if the fae didn't know he was a nobleman's son, he'd used the ring after dark, endangering the lives of the men who'd rescued him, and that showed a disrespect to his fellow Guardsmen that wasn't soon going to be forgotten.

A flash of red at the edge of my vision caught my attention and my pulse leaped with the sudden, desperate hope that it was Red. All thoughts of doing my job and keeping tabs on the novices were instantly gone and the memory of what it had felt like to be with her flooded me then swept away leaving me empty and cold.

Fuck.

I strained to drag my thoughts away from her. I couldn't think about her. Not here. Not now. Not ever.

Besides, it wasn't Red. It couldn't be her. There were no women, human or fae, in the Black Tower. The only woman who infrequently visited, was Rider's sister. She could communicate with animals and sometimes her mate, Flint, needed her help when one of our horses needed medical attention. But whenever she visited, Rider kept her away from the men, not just because he was an over-protective brother, but because she was a woman and this castle was filled with men who, unless they were fae-touched and enjoyed having sex with another man, only had contact with a woman on their lieu days.

The flash of red, did, however, come from the boy, Sawyer Herstind. He'd stepped out of the kitchen on the other side of the great hall, a tray in his hands containing his morning meal, and was trying to figure out where to sit. The men in front of him, a mix of human and fae, gave him a dark look then turned back to their meal, pointedly ignoring him.

Sawyer lifted his head and squared his shoulders. He was steeling himself against that and whatever else the men were going to throw at him, but it made him look even more like a haughty nobleman.

"Look at him," Bramwell hissed. "He doesn't even know he fucked up the other night. Bet it pisses him off that no one calls him 'my lord' anymore."

"The Lord Commander should have given him more than a rotation of stable duty," a man on the bench behind me murmured.

"Hard work would do him some good," someone else replied.

"So we toughen him up and teach him respect," Mikel said. "We can't have the other Guardsmen thinking there's something wrong with our group of novices."

A large human walked out of the kitchen and bumped Sawyer, making him slosh his ale half onto the piece of bread on his tray and half over one hand. The man shot Sawyer a dirty look and said something, but I was too far away to hear him. Those around me snickered and murmured about him not knowing his place or being stupid or selfish.

The boy's posture tightened even more and for a second it looked like he was going to drop his gaze — something he'd done a lot yesterday — but this morning he kept his head high. Guess he'd made a decision last night to stand up for himself. I could only hope that whatever the rest of the Guardsmen and Mikel had in store for him, he'd stay strong.

And while yes, it was my job to make sure no one killed themselves or killed anyone else, it was still always best if problems were worked out between the men.

Sawyer needed to stand up for himself as well as prove to the others that he understood the nature of his mistake. He also needed to prove that he was going to be a useful member of the Guard even though we had to keep him whether we liked him or not.

There was a fine balance between maintaining discipline and comradery and given that the humans spent the rest of their lives together with no way to leave, Rider almost always erred on the side of comradery... if it didn't endanger anyone's life.

Someone by the main doors caught the boy's attention and he started to hurry away from the dark looks and cold-shoulders the other Guardsmen were giving him then he slowed his pace to a fast, stately stride. He reached his goal and sat stiffly beside Lewin and across from Kit and Payne.

Talon had mentioned he'd asked the elite team to keep an eye on the boy. After discovering he was attracted to other men, Talon hoped that seeing Kit and Payne — two fae who'd recently taken mating vows with each other and were public with their affection — would eventually make Sawyer feel more comfortable with himself, since the humans didn't approve of males coupling.

"I can't believe one of the elite teams has welcomed him to their table," Bramwell said.

"My older brother said Talon told them to," Mikel replied. "They probably think if they don't, the Lord Commander will keep them stuck as a three man team doing daytime patrols to keep the traders that move between the Tower and the ring safe."

"But why would Talon do that? He knows what the runt did," Hamelin asked.

Durand huffed and rolled his eyes as if the answer was obvious. "The Captain of the Gold Tower likes his boys pretty and small like a girl. He's probably got his eye on the runt."

Wonderful. Talon was going to love hearing that

rumor. Yes, he'd slept with a lot of people, human and fae alike, but not children, and the only Guardsman I knew he was sleeping with at the moment was Quill.

Now he'll definitely keep his distance from Sawyer, which meant the boy was going to lose an ally, something he was already short on. Kit's team was going to be switching rotations soon and that meant there wasn't going to be anyone in the great hall for Sawyer to eat with.

"If Talon has his eye on him, he'll get special treatment for sure," Mikel said around a mouthful of bread. "The Lord Commander has already shown he won't do what's necessary to discipline the runt which means it's our responsibility to make sure he knows his place and doesn't get us killed."

"But what does that mean?" I asked. I really didn't like the direction the conversation was going. "I doubt the Lord Commander will like it if we put the boy in the infirmary."

"Don't tell me you haven't had a good disciplinary thrashing," Bramwell said to me. "You're already a soldier. You know what I'm talking about."

And even though I wasn't really a soldier, I did know. Discipline came in many forms. Rider wasn't usually a fan of beating someone — since it was far too easy for him to lose control — but he would if necessary. He preferred hard work and if we didn't need Sawyer and the other skilled novices in the rotation as soon as possible to get our ranks closer to full, I suspected the boy would be mucking out the stables all day for the rest of the season.

"And no one here is talking about sending him to the infirmary," Mikel added. "But just because he's small, doesn't mean we should go easy on him. He needs to learn what it's like to fight for real and he needs to know the rest of us won't stand by and let him risk our lives."

Which if they didn't break Sawyer's spirit or his body would actually be good for him. He'd grow stronger, gain valuable fighting experience, and if he took what they gave out, he'd earn the rest of the Guardsmen's respect.

Except they were going to be walking a fine line and I needed to join in just enough to keep myself in the group. If they pushed me out, I wouldn't be able to stop them from going too far until it was too late.

CHAPTER 8
Sage

My second full day at the Black Tower was just as exhausting as the first and even harder because I had woken sore and stiff from the previous day. The bruise I'd gotten from my stepfather's beating was now a deep dark purple and hurt even when I brushed my fingers against it.

It had taken everything I'd had to tightly wrap the scraps from my old dress around my chest to flatten my thankfully small breasts then drag on the rest of my too-big Black Guard uniform.

Kit, Payne, and Lewin had chatted with me during the morning meal, acting as if they weren't aware of the dark looks I was getting, and I'd tried to pretend I didn't notice as well.

I'd woken feeling amazing and boneless and a little heartbroken that I couldn't return to the Garden again to see Fantasy Man — or rather *be with him* since I hadn't actually seen him.

But not being able to see him was for the best. I'd almost let myself be distracted by how comfortable and safe I felt in his arms, and how much I yearned to stay with him, something I now had to forget about.

I had to focus on being Sawyer and staying strong no matter what happened and that started this morning.

Against everything I'd been taught as a woman, I had squared my shoulders, raised my chin, and decided my first full day at the Black Tower was the last day I looked at my feet and demurred to any man.

For now, in the Black Tower — at least until they caught me — I *was* a man. I could make eye contact without being punished, I could show off my fighting abilities, and I could ask questions of the men around me, including my superiors.

But by the time the day ended and I'd dragged my aching body up two flights of stairs to my room, I was exhausted.

Being brave and standing my ground was not just physically exhausting but emotionally as well. Mucking out the stalls that morning had been more difficult than yesterday because my body just didn't want to move. I'd also been tripped down the same hill on the running trail where I'd been tripped yesterday, despite trying to avoid the other novices.

Then they'd all gotten a great laugh at how pathetic I was at riding and fighting from horseback — since my step-father, Edred, hadn't allowed me to ride for years, men rode differently than women, and I'd never been taught how to fight or shoot a bow while on a moving animal.

To top it off, Talon had barely said more than a few words to me the entire time we were being tested and my emotions kept leaping between disappointment that he was ignoring me and no longer supporting me to thrilled that he wasn't going to use his magic on me and reignite my desperate desire for sex.

And while the memory of my beaten, dead body lying in the mist was burned into my mind's eye, I was just too sore and tired to even think about trying to become a better fighter in order to save my life.

I could only pray I adjusted to this new life quickly so I had time to prepare, since I had no idea when my vision was going to come true.

Using the pump and basin in my room and the soap and towels I'd taken from the bathhouse beneath the barracks, I scrubbed myself down, redressed, and collapsed onto my bed.

Tomorrow would be a better day.

I huffed. That was just wishful thinking. Tomorrow would be as sore and exhausting as today, and I just needed to fight through it. My brother's life was on the line and I had to hold out until he'd left the Great Five Kingdoms.

No, I *would* hold out. And I *would* survive whatever attack was coming my way.

For once, my life was my own. I controlled my destiny and I'd be damned if things went back to the way they'd been.

My eyes fluttered open — I hadn't realized I'd closed them — but instead of seeing the shadow of the pump and basin against the wall of my tiny room in the Black Tower, I saw a small pool of softly rippling water reflecting speckled starlight.

My pulse tripped. I was in the fae's garden. Again.

A mix of hope and fear and confusion twisted in my stomach.

I didn't belong here. I shouldn't have come here the last two nights and it didn't make sense that I'd be in the Garden again. I'd been certain — hoping? — those first two times had been a mistake, except here I was again.

Then my pulse tripped for a whole other reason.

I could be with Fantasy Man again.

My chest tightened knowing that was a bad idea even as my body throbbed in anticipation. We could make love again and I could feel that incredible rush I'd felt the last two times he'd made me come. So long as I didn't let myself forget my purpose in the real world—

Someone cleared his throat, the sound low and masculine. Another strange rush of hope swept through me. Lord Rider— No, here in the Garden he was *just* Rider. He'd been waiting for me last night.

I jerked my gaze to the bench on the other side of the pool, but it wasn't Rider waiting for me this time. It was the two fae who'd found me the first time I'd appeared in the Garden.

They sat side by side, watching me with the same heated, hungry gazes they'd had before, sending a cold shiver of uncertainty and worry oozing down my spine.

They were opposites of each other, one with black hair and black eyes and the other with white hair and yellow eyes, and were both stunningly beautiful. Their waist-length hair hung loose with only a few braids at their temples to keep it from their eyes as well as to show off their delicately pointed ears, and they didn't wear jerkins, only shirts, made from a thin material that hugged their sculpted, muscular physiques.

They were everything the minstrels' tales said a fae man was supposed to be: gorgeous, magical, with bejeweled eyes, and flowing hair, and oh-so-dangerous.

Black Hair's gaze locked on me and his mouth curled into a predatory smile. It was similar to the look Rider had given me last night, but while Rider's had called to something within me, excited me, this man's look just made me more nervous.

"Welcome to the Garden," he purred.

"We were hoping you'd come back," White Hair added, his expression also blatantly hungry for me.

Black Hair stood and started around the pool toward me. "I'm Wells and this is Crane. Are you ready to be entertained?"

I scrambled to my feet. It was bad enough most fae towered over me when I was standing, I didn't want to be caught on the ground and forced to have to crane my neck to look up up up at either of them.

"We've asked the others and it seems Rider didn't show you around the Garden the last two nights," White Hair, Crane, said, approaching from the other side, his expression just as hungry as Black Hair's— or rather Wells's. "We'd love to be your guides tonight, give you a proper introduction to all its... pleasures."

I took a step back, instinct sliding my gaze to my feet as I'd been instructed when a man approached me—

Jeez. I'd managed to keep my eyes up all day and now I was right back to being a "proper woman."

Except it had been easy to remember I could stand firm while in pants and a jerkin and with my hair cut short like a man's and a sword at my hip. Here, back in a dress and looking and feeling like I did before I'd taken Sawyer's place in the Black Guard, it was hard to ignore a lifetime of being told how to behave.

That, and everyone here *thought* I was a woman. I

had to behave like one if I didn't want to draw anyone's suspicion since I wasn't supposed to be here in the first place. I couldn't afford being caught and punished here or in the Black Tower.

Except hadn't Rider said something to his sister that first night about putting those children — or rather *men* — in their place. Were women here allowed to talk back and even make demands of the men around them?

I didn't know anything about fae women or even fae culture only that this Garden was a sacred place for them and humans were magically prevented from entering it.

"Come," Wells said, sliding his fingers down my arm and reaching for my hand.

I took another tentative step away from him, the urge to move farther twisting my insides. But my years of *instruction* kept me from fleeing. Running away would just make the punishment worse... except would there be a punishment here?

I didn't understand why Wells's look made me uncomfortable when Rider's hadn't. Although Rider's look hadn't been completely sexual like Wells's was, more... possessive, which should have terrified me even more. Fantasy Man had also exuded a sense of hungry desire for me and I'd still felt safe with him, desired having sex with him again, even knowing now that he wasn't a dream.

“We’ll get something to eat first,” Crane said, “then stroll through the gardens and make our way to the pools.”

“I appreciate the offer…” Would they go away if I just said no or would that make them angry?

They were both bigger and stronger than me and I didn’t have a weapon. I didn’t stand a chance against them in a fight, and I didn’t know if I *could* fight back. I hadn’t been able to with Edred and I wouldn’t have been able to with any human man.

I needed to come up with an excuse that convinced them I wasn’t available without angering them. “I’m ah…”

CHAPTER 9
Sage

"I'm meeting someone," I said praying that the excuse was a good enough and it wouldn't anger Wells or Crane.

Crane's yellow eyes narrowed. "Rider?"

"Yes," I lied.

Everyone seemed afraid of Rider. The two fae I'd overheard in the stables yesterday, the ones who'd made me realized the Garden hadn't been a dream, had been afraid Rider was courting me and would hurt anyone who got in his way.

I didn't think Rider was interested in me, not like these men were, but that didn't mean I couldn't make Wells and Crane think he was.

The encounter with Rider last night had been confusing to say the least. I'd thought he was trying to be friendly, but asking him to show me the Garden had somehow crossed a line I hadn't known was there.

I'd have rather used Fantasy Man to get Wells and Crane to back off, since I knew he was actually interested in me, but I still didn't know Fantasy Man's name.

Maybe I'd be able to get it tonight. Maybe tonight he'd feel comfortable letting me look at him... because it had been clear by the way we interacted that he hadn't wanted me seeing him.

No, Rider was my best choice. They'd figure out eventually that he wasn't interested, but maybe that would buy me enough time to learn how to deal with them or how to stop waking up in the Garden.

The thought of not returning made my stomach roil, even though coming here was dangerous and distracting and I shouldn't be doing it.

"Why would you want to spend time with him? I bet all he talks about is killing shadows and Guardsmen rotations. I doubt he knows how to properly treat a woman." Wells grabbed my hand before I could step away again and tugged me to his side, wrapping an arm around my waist to hold me close. "Spend time with us. I guarantee we'll make it enjoyable."

I tried to push against him and put space between us but he held tight. "But Rider—"

"You can make Rider wait. He'll understand," Crane said, drawing close and turning me slightly, boxing me in between him and Wells, Wells at my front, Crane at my back. "You'll take at least three mates, probably four..." He trailed his fingers along my neck, drawing heat, a hint of light, and an unwanted ache between my thighs.

"We'll be good opposites to grumpy, old Rider," Wells purred, then he dropped his voice to a conspiratorial whisper. "We'll help you tame his beast."

Crane chuckled, the sound dark and sensual, making my unwanted desire throb stronger, while everything else within me said, "no no no."

I didn't want to tame Rider's beast... well...

The memory of that intense look last night sent a shiver rushing through me.

"You like that?" Wells asked.

A part of me did like that. Except I sure as hell didn't want to do it with Wells and Crane.

Wells hooked a finger under my chin, tipped my head back, and lowered his lips close to mine. I shied back to avoid the kiss, but that only pressed me against Crane and I was suddenly very aware of his erection digging into my rear.

My pulse pounded, roaring in my ears. They were too close, too dangerous, and I had to get away. Now. His lips were drawing nearer and he'd captured my chin between his thumb and forefinger and I couldn't turn away.

"I'm not sure it would be wise to keep Rider waiting," I said in a rush, stopping him before he made contact with my lips. "I've just met him, but he doesn't strike me as a man you want to upset."

"Between us we're powerful enough to handle one wolf," Crane murmured, wrapping his large hand around the back of my neck, securing me even more in their grip.

"But—" Shadows, there had to be a way to get them to let me go. I could knee Wells in the groin, but Crane would grab me before I could attack him.

No, Rider, was still my best excuse. Those men in the stables had said they weren't going to court me because they feared Rider would act like Blaze had when he'd been courting Lark. They'd said Blaze had almost killed two of her other suitors before the Goddess bonded him to her.

"Remember Blaze?" I asked. "Blaze almost killed Lark's other suitors," I added.

Wells' eyes narrowed and he thankfully didn't finish the kiss. "How do you know about Blaze?"

"Lark warned me," I lied and I prayed to the Great Father that neither of these men were friends with Lark or her mates. "She said her brother will be worse than Blaze and I should be careful about who else I spend time with."

"If Rider has his sights on her..." Crane said, inching away from me. "He can be her first mate. She'll still take at least two more."

I wasn't going to take any, but I also wasn't stupid

enough to say that out loud. I didn't know why they thought I was in the market for a mate or even three mates, but I'd just gotten free of a man who controlled my life, I wasn't going back to that.

"He's going to have to let her follow the call of her marks," Wells shot back, his attention on Crane behind me.

"And he will once he's been bound to her." Crane took a full step away from me and I hurried a few steps away from Wells. "His blood lust will diminish once he's mated. And if he's set on her, he'll have the blood lust. Together we're more magically powerful than him, but he kills shadows for a living."

The muscles in Wells' jaw flexed, then he turned his hungry gaze back to me. "I'm not afraid of Rider, but I'd hate for him to interrupt our fun tonight."

He turned and strode up the path to the courtyard. Crane shot me an equally hungry look, then hurried after his friend, while I ran in the opposite direction. I didn't want to risk them changing their mind and I didn't want to run into anyone else.

I raced to the magical grove with the softly-lit passages and bedrooms and nooks, and went to the nook where I'd met Fantasy Man.

The space was empty and dark, just like the bedroom the nook peered into, and my chest tightened with disappointment.

It was ridiculous to think Fantasy Man would be

waiting for me, but I'd really hoped he would be. I'd hoped I'd shown him last night that he could trust me, that he was as safe with me as I felt with him and he'd open up a little bit more.

But maybe last night had been it for us.

He'd told me I'd had to go and I'd confirmed that when I'd realized I didn't belong in the Garden with him.

Maybe he'd known that from the start and that's why he hadn't wanted to tell me who he was.

I sagged into the bench, the aching desire Crane had awakened with his touch thrumming within me. It wasn't the desperate need Talon had inspired and I didn't feel as if I was going to burn up if I didn't release the pressure, but it was enough to make me acutely aware that now that I'd had sex and knew how incredible it was, I didn't want to stop.

The thought swirled my desire stronger but also added in a whisper of frozen fear.

I didn't desire Wells or Crane, but with one touch against the strange marks encircling my neck, Crane had made my body crave him. He'd said I'd have to follow the call of my marks, and I didn't like that my marks didn't seem to care who I had sex with or that they seemed to be connected with taking at least three mates and binding me to them.

But would that even happen? I wasn't really fae.

No. Being bound to a fae man was impossible.

Crane's touch hadn't turned me on because he'd touched my marks, but because after having sex with Fantasy Man and feeling Talon's magic, any kind of touch turned me on.

My marks weren't real and the marks weren't compelling me to find my mates.

That said, I needed to learn as much as I could about the fae and this garden, at least until I could figure out how to stop waking up here every night.

And as much as that thought hurt, because it meant I wouldn't be with Fantasy Man again or have Rider treat me with kindness, it was for the best. I was already lying to everyone in the Black Tower, I couldn't lie to everyone in the Garden as well. It was just too much.

CHAPTER 10

Sage

I WOKE with a throat and chest tight with regret but still determined to stay focused on my goal: keep my secret until Sawyer was safe and learn everything I could about the fae and the Garden and how to stop manifesting there.

My body hurt as much as it had yesterday and I pushed through getting dressed and headed down to the great hall for the morning meal.

I grabbed my usual bowl of porridge, rasher of bacon, slice of bread, and mug of watered ale, but when I got to the end of the long counter separating those getting their meal from the rest of the kitchen, I was disappointed to see there were no oranges.

I'd been unable to resist the luxury of the expensive fruit and had enjoyed an orange at every meal since I'd been at the Black Tower, but it didn't surprise me that they were out. The fruit came from the Southern Isles which were weeks away from the closest fae ring which made them difficult to get in most of the Great Five Kingdoms. Only the wealthiest in the kingdoms could afford them and I'd been shocked to see them at the Tower since no one here was wealthy — and if they had been, they weren't anymore.

Lewin, a good-natured man with a shaved head, blue eyes, deeply tanned complexion, and someone who didn't seem to care that I'd screwed up the other night, caught my attention from his seat in the middle of the great hall.

I dodged out of the way of a man purposefully trying to bump into me — having learned my lesson yesterday during all three meals — and joined him.

The rest of the guardsmen continued to give me dark looks and hissed snide comments to one another, but, like I'd also done yesterday, I held my head high and was determined to pretend I didn't notice.

There wasn't anything I could do about it. All I could do was work hard and hope they'd eventually forget about me.

"No orange this morning?" Payne asked as he sat on the bench across from me.

He was an enormous fae, one of the biggest at the Tower and had two large swords sheathed at each hip

— armed, like all the other Guardsmen were armed, even though we were eating.

"Not this morning," I replied as Kit, his bonded mate and a member of their four-man elite hunting team, settled in beside him.

Kit was beautiful, just like all fae, including Payne, and was almost as tall as his mate, but had a fraction of his girth. He was thin, lean-muscled, and probably the perfect person to teach me the fighting techniques I needed to survive my impending death since the fighting style that best suited our bodies were similar despite our height difference.

Except that really wasn't what I should be asking him about. I hurt too much to ask for extra training, and with my additional half shift of stable duties after the evening meal, I didn't have any extra time.

But after last night's unexpected reappearance in the Garden, I *should* ask him about that.

Learning about the Garden didn't require me to be in any kind of physical condition or have spare time. We could do it while we ate... if I could figure out how to bring up the topic without drawing anymore attention to myself than I already had by screwing up the other night and by just plain being a nobleman's son.

"Guess we'll get to see your real hair color," Lewin drawled, making Kit and Payne laugh. "It's the oranges keeping your hair orange, isn't it?"

I rolled my eyes at him but laughed with them.

"Maybe if you start eating them, you'll actually get some hair."

"Even more incentive to avoid the things," Lewin chuckled, running a hand over his head. "The ladies like the smooth top, say it's sexy."

Payne snorted, his striking amethyst eyes sparkling with mirth. "They say that because you're paying them to say that."

"And it's worth every bit. Do you know how hard it is to listen to you two go at it every night and know I've got one more day until I can see my sweet Vreni?"

"Are you denying us our newly mated bed?" Kit asked, batting his eyelashes at Lewin. "You can always join us."

"Sounds good to me," Payne added, shocking me.

The minstrels' tales said the fae were more sexual than humans — which I'd seen first hand in the Garden — but Kit and Payne were married... unless a fae's bonding didn't mean the same thing as a human's marriage.

Lewin yanked off a small piece of his bread and tossed it at Payne. "You two are pretty and all, but I like someone soft and sweet and nice smelling when I fuck her."

"And you really can't complain." Payne tossed the bread back. "We've spent the last two nights in the Garden so you can get your beauty sleep."

I fought the urge to sit forward and look overeager. This was my opening.

"What's it like?" I asked.

"Glorious, when those two aren't going at it like the newly weds they are," Lewin laughed. "I dream of Vreni's big tits and her soft skin, and sunshine. Man, I can't wait for you novices to get into the rotation so we can get our regular lieu time back. There's daytime in the Gray, but hardly ever sunshine."

Which was depressing to learn, but made sense as to why this place between realms where the Three Gates of the Realms met was called the Gray. The two days I'd been here it had been overcast and misty all day and now, from what Lewin said, it seemed like that was the Gray's natural state.

And wasn't at all what I wanted to talk about. "I didn't mean your beauty sleep. I mean the Garden."

"Why do you want to know?" Lewin replied, popping the piece of bread in his mouth that he'd thrown at Payne and Payne had thrown back to him. "You can't go there."

"I don't know," I said with a shrug, focusing on my porridge. "Half of the Guard is fae, but I know nothing about your people. Up until yesterday, I thought all fae had magic."

"I'm kind of surprised you humans still believe that," Payne said.

He'd told me yesterday that he didn't have magic, which was why he'd said he wasn't eligible to have a mate… which brought up a whole bunch of other questions that I didn't know if I should ask or not.

How suspicious would I look if I pressed about mating details? Did men ask about things like that? They were more likely to talk about what it was like to have sex with a woman than to marry her, which could be an interesting perspective to learn but wouldn't help me navigate the social rules of the Garden.

"About half of us don't have any magic," Payne continued, "and of the half that do, most don't have particularly powerful magic."

"Although you could say your magic is your strength," Kit added, teasing his fingers through Payne's shoulder-length dark blond hair. "You're easily twice as strong as I am."

"My chest and arms are twice as big, lover. That's not magic. That's math," Payne shot back with a smile.

"And both of you are probably four or five times stronger than Sawyer, so he must think you're gods," Lewin chuckled.

"Ha ha," I replied. "No, I just think you're all really strong."

Lewin wrapped an arm around my neck, drew my head to his side, and ruffled my hair. I stiffened at the contact suddenly aware of how close his hand was to my chest, even though I wore my heavy jerkin and I doubted he'd be able to feel my breasts with an accidental brush.

"You'll get there, runt, don't worry," he laughed and let me go. "You're sixteen, so you're due for a growth spurt any day now. Then all the other novices will be looking up at you."

I snorted. That would never happen. Not the looking up at me or me getting taller, since I was twenty and as tall as I was ever going to get.

And this wasn't the conversation I wanted to have.

"Tell me about the Garden. I overheard some of the guys talking about a new arrival with all her marks," I pressed. "It seemed really important to them. They were really excited about it."

"It is important," Kit replied. "A new arrival is someone who's now a fae adult and can enter the Garden, either physically or spiritually. For men it just happens when we're about thirty. For women, it's when their mating marks first awaken which could be as early as twenty but usually around thirty or thirty-five."

"But it's kind of a raw deal for the women," Payne added around a mouthful of bacon. "Whether they're ready or not, the marks increase their sexual desire and compels them to find their mates. My sister was in the middle of her apprenticeship with a Water Master at the White Tower when her marks awakened and she couldn't concentrate until her first mate had been bound to her."

My pulse stuttered at that. *Increases their sexual desire and compels them?*

CHAPTER 11
Sage

WAS that what was happening to me? Were those strange marks compelling me to have sex?

I wanted to be with Fantasy man again and again and had been disappointed that I hadn't seen him last night which wasn't like me at all. I'd also been turned on when Crane had touch the marks on my neck even though everything within me told me he was dangerous.

I'd thought that was because Talon had used his magic on me and awakened my desires, but maybe my heightened sexual need wasn't his magic... or wasn't *all* from his magic.

Except I wasn't fae.

My ears were round, my eyes were boring and brown not jewel-toned, and I wasn't beautiful like all the fae I'd seen and especially not like Lark.

I was human through and through... alright, maybe I wasn't completely human. I had premonitions that had now become visions so I *was* fae-touched — the kind of fae-touched that meant I had a bit of magical ability, not the kind that meant I was a man attracted to other men. But being fae-touched didn't make me fae.

Except something was up because three times now I'd gone to sleep in the Black Tower and woken in the Garden.

"So what? She was set up with a guy, took the mating vows, and was fine?" Lewin asked.

"It's not that simple," Kit replied. "Our women take at least three mates. Payne's sister would have been better able to focus after taking her first mate, but she still would have been distracted for possibly years until she'd bound all her mates to her, however many that ended up being."

"Five," Payne added. "The Goddess blessed her with five. All with powerful magic."

"How does that work? In bed I mean?" Lewin cocked his head to the side as if he were trying to envision six people all having sex.

A shiver of need rushed through me. I didn't know what six people in bed looked like, but I sure knew what five did and it had been incredibly sexy.

I took a long gulp of ale, trying to hide my reaction, but it went down the wrong way and I ended up coughing and gasping. The others burst into laughter and Lewin slapped me on the back, doing nothing to help me catch my breath.

"I think you've broken him," Lewin laughed. "So she's set up with many guys and takes the vows."

"It's not just any guy, and we don't *set her up*," Kit said. "She finds men who please her. In fact our women are encouraged to embrace the compulsion of their marks and take as many men as she likes—"

"He means sex," Lewin said with a knowing wink to me as if I hadn't already figured out what he'd meant.

"But not like how you humans think of sex," Payne replied with a pointed glare at Lewin. "We see sex differently than you do. You control your desires and the desires of your women. You have all these rules about sex."

"If your women are lucky, they're allowed to marry for love," Kit added, his expression turning grim.

"Only if they're peasants," I said, the words slipping out before I could stop them.

Noblemen's daughters had no choice. They were sold for money and political power. That was all they were good for.

That was all *I'd* been good for.

And even though I'd only spent two days living as a man and was so sore it hurt to even think about moving, I felt freer magically bound to the Black Tower than I ever had at Herstind Castle.

"Your sister?" Lewin asked.

I blinked at him. I didn't think I'd told him about me, but I had told Talon and Lord Quill. I hadn't wanted to, but when Lord Quill had been ready to run back to Herstind Castle to rescue me, I'd had to say something. Guess one of the two had told Kit and his team.

"I think if our father was still alive he would have found a good match for her, but he died before a match was made and our step-father signed a marriage contract with one of his friends."

Lewin gave a knowing nod. "Marrying her into a friend's family is a good way to strengthen ties between the families."

I was painfully aware of that, but I got the impression he said that for Kit and Payne's benefit. Which made sense. If I didn't know much about fae and their culture, they might not know a whole lot about humans. Sure, the men of the Black Guard worked together, but that didn't mean they talked about their cultural differences. Especially the difference between men and women's relationships since all of the humans had been forced to leave their relationships and weren't allowed to be married.

"And it doesn't even have to be an heir," Lewin added. "Marrying her to any of his friend's sons would have helped solidified their family ties."

"Except my sister wasn't betrothed to his son. It was

him. He was a widower and she was to become his second wife as soon as she was able to bear children."

Which was also common among human nobility. Edred's second wife was younger than me and he was the same age as my father. The only reason I'd been saved the same fate was because my husband-to-be's heart had given out and he'd died before I could be shipped off to him.

"He died and his second son agreed to honor the contract and she was to be married to him when he returned from his sailing expedition," I added.

"That's just disgusting," Payne huffed. "She should get to choose, like our women do."

"Sort of do," Kit corrected. "A woman could have fallen madly in love with you, but you have no magic, so the Goddess wouldn't have chosen you to be her mate."

Lewin frowned. "So what? She sleeps with whoever strikes her fancy and then what—? Her mates are randomly selected from the group?"

"Pretty much," Kit said. "There has to be the possibility of love between the two, but a spark also needs to form between their soul magics. She doesn't have to have sex with a man to discover if he's fated to be hers, but it helps."

"And you have to have magic," Payne added. "A man without magic hasn't been mated for almost four hundred years."

"But that's why the fae you overheard talking about the new arrival were so excited," Kit said. "Our population is mostly male, so there aren't a lot of available females. One only shows up every five or six years. And while some mated women like to invite the odd unmated man to their beds, most are content with the mates they have."

"So you're saying you guys only get to have sex with a woman of your own kind when one is looking for her mates?" Lewin stared at them his expression stunned. "Not at any other time?"

"Not really," Kit replied.

"No wonder you encourage your women to sleep with everyone," Lewin said. "You must love that those marks make them horny."

Which explained why Wells and Crane had been so aggressive with me. Even if they didn't want to be mated, I was their only chance at having sex with a fae woman for who-knew-how-long. And while I felt a little bad for them, that wasn't enough for me to have sex with them. If I was going to be free of my real life while in the Garden, then *I* was going to choose who I had sex with, no one else.

My thoughts leaped to Fantasy Man and how incredible he'd made me feel. I wanted more of that, even if it wasn't real because I wasn't a real fae.

This was a chance I'd never have again. I could ask

any man in the Garden who struck my fancy and he'd probably say yes.

But would I have the courage to ask?

Asking for what I wanted went against everything I'd been taught. And really, I'd be lying to them. They'd be having sex with me with the hope that they'd become my mate, and because I wasn't a fae, that would never happen.

"But if you don't please her, she won't invite you into her bed," Kit reminded. "No matter how much she needs to have sex."

"So you have to treat her like a queen." Lewin gave a knowing nod.

My pulse stuttered. What if the fae's Goddess *did* bind me with the men I had sex with? They'd be furious to find out they were stuck with a human.

"You should treat any woman like a queen," Payne replied. "Even if you're paying her."

"Oh, I agree." Lewin sat back, his hands raised in submission. "You get way better service and extra perks if you treat your pleasure house girl with respect." Then he turned to me. "So that's your first lesson. You—"

No. I couldn't forget what I'd decided last night. I had to figure out how to stop going to the Garden. Period. And until I did, I had to avoid contact with everyone, even Fantasy Man.

"Hey, kid." Lewin ruffled my hair again, jerking my attention to him.

"What?"

The guys burst into laughter and I'd realized they'd said something to me.

"For sex. If you want better sex with the girls in Lehyrst," Lewin said, "you have to treat them like queens."

"Right. Of course."

Except I'd already had the best sex of my life and, shadows help me, I was going to do my damnedest never to have it again.

So long as Talon didn't use his magic on me to heighten my sexual attraction to him, I'd be fine. I could withstand whatever my fake marks were making me feel. The desire I'd felt when Crane had touched them had been my imagination, a remnant of Talon's magic, nothing more.

They weren't compelling me because I wasn't a fae woman in search of her mates.

CHAPTER 12
Sage

"JEEZ," Grefin said as he sat on the bench beside me, boxing me in with Lewin while the guys laughed at me. "Do you even know how to treat a woman like a queen?"

"I practiced on your mother," Lewin shot back as he reached over my tray and snatched a rasher of bacon from Grefin's plate.

"Hey." Grefin tried to grab it back, but Lewin leaned farther away, making Grefin huff but thankfully not push me aside to get to the other man. "Go to the kitchen and get me more, thief."

Lewin shoved the piece into his mouth. "Nope."

"Runt." Grefin turned his glare to me. "Go to the kitchen and get me more."

"Don't you dare," Kit replied before I could even

think of standing. "You're a big boy. You can get your own bacon."

"But the runt's so much quicker than I am. He'd be to the kitchen and back in a flash," Grefin huffed.

"If some asshole didn't trip him first," Payne said under his breath.

"Learning to dodge is a very important skill." Grefin squashed the rest of his bacon between two slices of bread and took a huge bite. "But that's not why I'm here. I've got good news, bad news, and great news."

Kit's eyes narrowed. "What's the bad news?"

"Frost's team ran across a pair of big cats and both Frost and Morys are on bedrest."

"Shadows," Payne hissed. "I thought the shadow cats were solitary. Even the big ones."

"So did they. So did all of us," Grefin replied, his expression turning grim.

"So," Kit asked, his tone hesitant, "what's the good news?"

"You're switched to nights starting tomorrow so today is now a lieu day for you guys."

"Nice! Vreni and sunshine here I come," Lewin whooped, making the men behind us chuckle and look back at him.

But their smiles vanished the second they saw me sitting beside him and I fought the urge to shrink back into myself and pretend I was invisible like a proper woman. Here, I was Sawyer Herstind, a boy—

No, I was bound to the Black Tower which meant I was a *man*. And even though it felt like I was painting myself in red by keeping my head up and making eye contact with the other men, I knew I'd draw less attention by doing so.

"And the great news," Grefin continued, "is that I'm your fourth for the rest of the rotation."

Payne grinned, reached over the table, and clasped Grefin's forearm. "That *is* great news." But then his smile faded and his gaze jumped to me. "But it means this will be our last meal together for the rest of the rotation. Probably longer."

Which meant I was no longer going to have allies in the great hall during mealtime.

Of course, given the reaction the other men had toward me, it was probably better if Kit, Payne, and Lewin stopped associating with me. I didn't want the other men to start treating them differently because of me.

"It was going to happen next rotation anyway," Grefin said with a shrug. "But with Frost's team out and Costin's team needing at least one rotation off nights so they don't go crazy—"

"Ours is the best hunter team to step up so long as Rider gives us a fourth." Kit gave me an apologetic smile. "Since we lost Hodge, we've been on days."

"For too damned long," Lewin said, his expression turning grim.

"The other hunter teams deserve a rest," Kit finished.

"I understand." In fact I was shocked they all — well everyone except Grefin — were upset that they wouldn't be able to continue eating meals with me. "I appreciate you offering to share your table for the meals we have had together."

Grefin snorted, waved his hand in the air and nodded his head in a mock bow. "Anything to please the lord."

I opened my mouth to insist that wasn't what I'd meant then snapped it shut. Talking back would get me punished.

No. Talking back would be like any other man here.

Why was that so hard to remember?

"There you go showing your peasant roots again," Lewin said with a laugh before I could think of an appropriate response. "You know he's not a lord anymore. You don't have to bow down to him."

"Stop acting like a lord and maybe the rest of us can forget you were one," Grefin shot back, his gaze jerking to the men behind us then back to me, reminding me of what I already knew: that the men of the Black Tower were determined to remind me that I wasn't special anymore. I was just like them.

Except I had no idea what I'd done that had made me look like a lord.

"You used a fancy phrase," Payne whispered, figuring out that I had no idea what Grefin was talking about. "And I heard you walked like a lord yesterday."

"Head held high, that kind of thing," Lewin added.

"Because people kept giving me grief about looking at my feet."

There wasn't any way I could win. I looked down, I was weak. I looked up, I was arrogant. They didn't want to like me and I shouldn't have cared if they did or not. It was all going to come crashing down sooner or later.

"They'll see you for who you are eventually," Payne said.

"Yeah, and who's that?" Grefin asked.

"A spark who's damned fast with a sword," Kit replied.

Grefin huffed. "Yeah, well. The runt is that. At least you're not terrible with a sword."

"Gee, thanks." I rolled my eyes at him, but suspected coming from Grefin that was a big compliment.

I didn't know him or anyone at the Black Tower very well yet — and the plan wasn't to ever get to know anyone well — but I had a feeling despite being gruff and grumpy, Grefin was a good man. I doubted Payne would be so happy to have him on their team if he hadn't been.

"Now if I don't want the stablemaster to hold me through lunch, I've got to get a head start on my duties." I grabbed my tray before the others could argue with me and hurried to the back of the great hall to put my dirty dishes in the bin by the kitchen door.

I still had time before I needed to be at the stables, and Kasen, the stablemaster, probably wouldn't make me work through lunch even though he'd complained about how slow I was yesterday.

But if I waited for the second bell that told everyone to go to their morning assignments, I'd get stuck in a crowd of men all putting their dishes in the bin, and I didn't want to get trapped among men who were all bigger and stronger than me *and* who didn't like me.

I reported to the stables and, as expected, Kasen put me straight to work shoveling soiled hay and horse shit from the stalls into a wheelbarrow, and wheeling it to the manure pile outside the Tower's walls.

I'd been sore and stiff before I'd started and by the time the fourth bell rang telling me it was time for lunch, I hurt even more. I'd thought Edred had made me work hard carrying buckets of water up the narrow stairs in Herstind Castle and scrubbing the floors. But now I was using muscles I'd never used before and still had that horrible bruise that Edred had given me that hurt with every little movement.

There weren't any oranges at the midday meal

either, but given that they hadn't had any at breakfast, that was understandable, except when I'd stepped out of the kitchen with my meal, I noticed the man sitting at the closest table had an orange… and so did the two men sitting with him.

Guess they'd had a few and I just hadn't gotten to the great hall early enough to grab one.

Two of the three men with the oranges shot me dark looks while the third picked up his fruit and gave it a small toss into the air, catching my attention. He flashed me a wicked smile, obviously pleased I'd noticed he had an orange, then dug his nail in and started peeling it.

I squared my shoulders, determined to ignore him, and headed down the closest aisle between the long benches and tables before someone behind me could bump me and make me slosh my ale.

As I moved, my gaze swept over those sitting and talking and laughing, searching for Kit, Payne, or Lewin before remembering I wasn't going to see them anymore.

More men shot me dark glares, while others picked up oranges and made a point of showing them to me.

My throat tightened. There were oranges everywhere when there hadn't been any in the kitchen. But I bet if I'd asked someone working on the other side of the counter if there'd been more, I'd have been told no, because this was another punishment.

The men had figured out — and damn quickly too — how much I loved oranges and had decided I didn't deserve any.

It shouldn't have hurt. It was just a piece of fruit, something I'd only had once before coming to the Black Tower, but it had been an unexpected bright spot in the last two days.

Except it wasn't being denied the orange that stung. It was the fact that this demonstration proved that with the exception of Kit and his elite hunting team, I had no other allies in the Black Guard and the rest of the men weren't just going to ignore me like I'd hoped.

Even Talon had avoided me yesterday, barely making eye contact when we were being tested on how well we could fight from horseback. And while a part of me had been grateful that I hadn't had to resist his magic that made me want to have sex with him — hell, sex with anyone and everyone — it hurt to know that he'd decided with the rest of the Guard that I was a spoiled nobleman who needed to be punished.

I could only pray that they'd stick with denying me oranges and just bumping me out of their way. That I could deal with.

Besides, life had been harder living in Herstind Castle with Edred. There I'd been afraid for Sawyer's life as well as my own and anything — the wrong look, the right look, just walking past Edred — could set him off and make him decide I or Sawyer needed to be disciplined.

CHAPTER 13

Sage

I FOUND a seat at the end of the table in the corner, as far away from the other men as I could get, and tried to look like I didn't care... which I knew made me look more like the haughty noble they thought I was. Now that I knew this was the way things were going to go, I'd make sandwiches and eat in my room. Maybe if I stayed out of sight, they'd get bored with me.

I ate as quickly as I could and got out of the great hall long before the fifth bell rang, desperate to get away from the dirty looks and sneered comments. It was still early but there wasn't any point in returning to my room in the barracks wing of the castle before the next bell rang, so I went out the pasture gate — avoiding the main gate and the men stationed there — and headed to the practice area where all the Black Guard novices were to meet for our afternoon training.

The Gray's perpetual mist curled around my feet and ankles, thicker today than the previous two days, and I stood, just to the right of the gate, staring at the jagged, rocky landscape stretched before me.

Today the fog was too thick, and I couldn't see the massive Shadow Gate towering in the distance, but I knew it was there, could somehow sense it this afternoon, with its ominous presence and threat of consuming darkness, when I hadn't been able to sense it the previous days.

Ahead, swathed in rolls of undulating mist, was the pasture, a great patch of dark green grass kept alive by fae magic so the horses could graze, and to my right was the laundry building with whisps of smoke curling from its chimneys that melted into the fog.

Beyond lay the practice area where men on the night shift or those on lieu time and not restricted to a schedule practiced with each other or at the archery range or the tiltyard on horseback.

The men laughed and called out to each other, a boisterous reminder that they were a team, a family of sorts, something I ached for.

Before Edred had manipulated the lottery, my family had become small. Just me and Sawyer. Our parents and middle brother were dead and we were strangers in our own home, living with a stepfather who saw Sawyer as a weak, sickly stepson who he didn't want to have as his heir, and me as a means of gaining money to fund his lavish lifestyle and a way of securing more political strength by marrying me off.

But the men at lunch had made it clear that I wasn't one of them even though — if I'd actually been Sawyer — I'd have had no choice in staying because once someone was bound to the Black Tower, the only way to leave was through death.

And I needed to remember that I never would belong.

Eventually they'd discover the truth and that would be that. I wouldn't be able to keep up the disguise of being a boy forever.

The pasture door swung open, startling me, and Lord Rider, the Lord Commander of the Black Guard, strode out with two rucksacks slung over his shoulder.

"You're early," he said, his voice edged with a chilling hardness that made my chest ache even as I fell into his stunning silver eyes, hoping to see a glimmer of the kindness I'd seen when he'd met me in the Garden the other night.

"Here." He held out one of the bags. "Be useful."

I took it, staggered a bit under it's weight — *what the hell is in here? Rocks?* — and scrambled to catch up to him.

"You disappointed me yesterday," he said without looking back at me as he strode to the practice area and the two jagged boulders marking the entrance to the running trail. "I'd thought, being a lord and all, you'd be better at fighting from horseback."

And from the way everyone had laughed at me, I was sure they'd all expected me to excel at fighting from horseback, too.

Thankfully, very few of the human novices had done well at it. Even Hamelin and Ambrose who'd been soldiers before their names had been drawn, had done badly.

"You should have at least managed to hit the target with your arrow," he said.

"Yes, my lord," I murmured, my cheeks heating with shame that I'd instinctually fallen back on my old, feminine habits *and* that I'd missed the target yesterday.

I should have made that shot, but I hadn't timed my release properly or compensated for how my body moved when the horse was cantering. I also hadn't wanted to take a long time setting up my shot like I had during my archery test.

As a result. I'd completely missed the target. Didn't even hit the hay and made everyone howl with laughter.

Lord Rider reached the boulders and dropped his bag. It hit the ground with a heavy thud that sounded an awful lot like rocks.

He leveled his silver glare on me, sending a shiver

of unwanted desire rushing down my spine and making my thoughts stutter in shock.

Yes he was beautiful, but I wasn't under the influence of Talon's magic anymore. I shouldn't have had that reaction to him.

But as much as I'd hoped that was true, there was something about him that drew my attention whether I wanted to look at him or not. Just like there was something about Lord Quill.

I heaved my gaze away from him, dropping it to my feet, then jerking it to the mouth of the running trail — because I *had* to stop looking at my feet!

But Talon crested the rise as I heaved my attention up and my pulse stalled completely.

Shadows he was breathtaking!

His long, white hair swished behind him with his movement, a shock of light against his all-black Guardsman uniform — a uniform that covered what I knew was a stunning, sculpted body.

The memory of him naked, droplets of water sliding over those perfect muscles, drawing my attention down down down to his large cock, swept through me, and the ache between my thighs, that I'd thought had eased, surged back to life.

Heat raced up my neck and across my face with desire and embarrassment, and I fought the urge to throw myself at him.

Great Father. I wished I'd never stumbled across

him in the bath, never saw his incredible body, and never felt the power of his magic that ignited a desire I hadn't even known I had.

I'd thought a day of him ignoring me would have been enough. I hadn't felt this way when he'd been standing on the other side of the practice yard avoiding me.

But it was once again like it had been two days ago after I'd lost my fight with Lord Rider. Talon had turned his mesmerizing gaze on me, his eyes a captivating swirl of pink, purple, blue, and gold, and my whole body had throbbed with desire for him.

He'd known it and he'd used it to try to get me to take my shirt off to prove I wasn't seriously injured. And while a part of me had screamed in panic, the rest of me had begged to let him touch me, satisfy me, fill me like Fantasy Man had filled me.

Talon stumbled to a halt, just before crossing the threshold from the trail to the practice yard, his attention frozen on me and my flaming-red face.

Then the mist around him billowed, rushing up his legs and around his hands and face. It grew dark, transforming from mist into shadows, and bled into his soft, pale eyes, turning them black.

"Fuck." Lord Rider hissed and lunged for Talon as a wave of darkness exploded from Talon's body and slammed into me.

CHAPTER 14
Sage

Darkness poured into my chest as if my clothes and skin didn't mean anything to the power rushing out of Talon. It seized my muscles, immobilizing me with my head thrown back, my mouth open on a scream I couldn't release, and flooded me with a soul-freezing cold.

Lord Rider slashed at it with his daggers. It screeched inside my head, the same horrifying sound the shadow monsters had made when I'd first came through the fae ring and they'd surrounded me.

Except this shadow monster's cry was louder and edged with knives. It sliced into my soul, sending frozen agony screaming through me and stealing what little breath I had left.

Talon took a shaky step forward as if he wasn't in

control of his body and a shadow tendril swatted at Lord Rider. He jerked out of the way, slicing into it and sending more screeching agony shooting through me.

My muscles convulsed, and I released a strange, strangled scream, before the muscle-freezing cold took hold of me again.

I mentally heaved against its grip, desperate to break free, to end the cold, to — Great Father! — just breathe. Darkness swarmed across my vision, but I couldn't tell if it was from lack of air or shadow enveloping my eyes like it enveloped Talon's.

"Let him go, Talon," Lord Rider growled.

"No," Talon replied— No, a shadow. It was a shadow controlling Talon, making his voice sound strange, like gravel and darkness and ice and... heartache? "Hungry."

The shadow jerked me forward and Talon wrapped one hand around my back, capturing me against him, and tangled the other in my hair. He yanked my head back and sudden, desperate need erupted into the cold.

Now my body, still locked in ice, begged for a release, for Talon's mouth on mine, his hands caressing and fondling, his cock driving into me, bringing me to the heights of unimaginable pleasure.

The shadow inside me whirled stronger, building up my need. Its screeches turned to moans, its hunger aching and overwhelming.

It was starving. I didn't know how or why, but it needed something from me, something I wanted to give it—

No. I didn't want to give it whatever it craved. It was consuming me. I could feel it devouring my strength along with my desire, pulling on my soul, pushing in its ice, too much ice. I was cold, so cold.

"Fuck, Talon." Lord Rider sliced at Talon's arm.

The shadow batted his hand away, but Lord Rider countered with the dagger in his other hand, faster than the shadow could respond, and slammed the blade into Talon's shoulder, drawing a strangled cry of pain.

The shadow screeched, the horrible sound ringing in my ears, my head— hell, my whole body, while frozen agony exploded through my chest. Then Talon crushed his mouth against mine, oblivious to the dagger in his shoulder, and my core spasmed with a sudden, powerful release.

Stars flashed behind my eyes, my essence whirling with pleasure. It was almost as incredible as the releases Fantasy Man had given me and would have been incredible if we'd had more time and less clothes and I hadn't been freezing.

The shadow surged into every crevasse of my being, filling me with ice and heartache and hunger. I wanted to sob at its pain, at its terrible need, but I was trapped within myself, frozen, my body desperate to be free, to breathe.

It captured something within me, some spark infused in the very essence of my being, whirled it into a brilliant, blinding vortex, and yanked it out of my mouth into Talon's.

A bone-deep cold flooded in where the vortex had been, leaving me trembling, and yet still throbbing with need, satisfied and yet begging from more — *please more* — even as I coughed and gasped for air.

Talon groaned and the darkness sank under his skin and bled out of his eyes. He stared at me, his expression stunned for a moment as if he didn't know what had just happened, then his beautiful, pale eyes widened with horror.

"Oh, Goddess," he gasped.

Lord Rider snarled, yanked me out of Talon's grasp, and rammed his fist into Talon's face. Talon staggered back and I fell to my knees, my body weak and trembling, unable to hold me up.

"Oh Goddess, no." Talon's wide-eyed gaze locked on me, his expression horrified and shocked. "You're fae-touched."

"You already knew that," Lord Rider growled. "Take another step back."

"No. The other one, too. You taste like a fae." He took an unsteady step toward me, and Rider's growl deepened with warning.

My desire flared stronger as if he hadn't just made me come with his magic, and I dropped my head, gasping and fighting the all-too-feminine moan of pleasure that bubbled in my throat.

"What's your magic?" Talon asked.

"Not the conversation we should be having," Rider snapped. "Is it satisfied or do I need to stab you again?"

"It's under control." Talon's boots inched closer as if he couldn't help himself, despite Rider's snarling, and my breath turned ragged.

I wanted Talon now as much as I'd wanted him when his shadow had possessed me. I wanted to feel that pressure and desire again and again despite the pain and the cold—

Shadows! I needed to get away, relieve the pressure building inside me. *Please, Great Father.* Except I wasn't even sure I could stand, let alone run away... not that I could run away without permission.

Talon reached for me, and I tried to scramble back but couldn't get my limbs to move properly and ended up flailing and slamming my butt against the hard ground. Tears burned my eyes, and my face was on fire with embarrassment as Rider rammed his shoulder into Talon and shoved him back.

"It's not under control," I ground out, fighting to keep my voice pitched low. "What did you do to me?"

"Something he shouldn't have." He glared at Talon. "Stay the hell away from him." Then he grabbed my chin and jerked my attention up to him. My need surged stronger. Why did all the fae have to be so damned beautiful? "Fuck, his pupils are still blown. You were supposed to get your *magic* under control last night, Talon."

Except the moment Rider said it, I knew what had happened hadn't been because of Talon's magic, it had been because of the shadow inside him, and it had been desperate and hungry... and lonely.

My thoughts stuttered at that. How the hell did I know it was lonely, that its hunger was born from a need to be filled with something it hadn't gotten, or hadn't gotten enough of, in a long time? And all it had, all that was helping it hold on, was its connection with Talon.

It wasn't malicious or evil, it was like the shadows cast on a sunny day, neither good nor bad. It just was. Just another creature trying to survive.

The realization shook me. The shadow monsters that had attacked me when I'd come through the ring had tried to kill me. I didn't know if that made them evil or just wild animals. But everything I'd heard about the shadow monsters said they were evil. Except the shadow in Talon wasn't. I knew that in the depth of my soul.

"I'm sorry, Sawyer," Talon said. "My... *magic* feeds on... *feelings*—"

"Sex," I corrected, forcing my gaze up to meet his, my trembling, frozen, aching exhaustion making me bold beyond my good sense. "Your *shadow* feeds on *sex.*"

Talon shot a worried look at Rider.

"It's not a shadow," Rider said.

"It is." A shudder of cold mixed with need swept through me. "It's so hungry, so... lonely."

Talon's eyes widened. "How do you know that? No one else feels that when it feeds. Not even other fae."

"Could have been the force of the attack," Rider said. "Has it ever fed like that before? I thought you needed actual sex to feed it."

"So did I," Talon replied. "Definitely an orgasm."

The heat in my face that had been starting to fade roared back to life, a sharp burning contrast on my cheeks, ears, and neck to the cold buried within me.

"Well, fuck," Rider huffed. "I thought because you're still being affected by his allure that you didn't come." He ran his hands through his hair, mussing his topknot and not noticing... and making himself even more breathtaking. "This is a fucking mess. You—" He glared at Talon. "You need to get to the infirmary and get that looked at and get away— Fuck. I need you with the novices. I can't afford to send you back to the Gold Tower until we've at least finished this rotation."

"It's satisfied," Talon replied, shooting me a sad

look filled with apology that only made my need blaze hotter. “It won’t need to feed for at least the rest of the rotation, probably longer.”

“Fine, but you’re still off for the rest of the day.” Rider turned to glare at me. “And you need to get into the bushes and jerk off so you can concentrate.”

CHAPTER 15
Sage

"I WHAT?" I squeaked.

"Go down the trail to the trees, find yourself some privacy, and deal with that." He gave a pointed look at my crotch that made my breath hitch.

"I'm not going into the forest and—" Great Father, how would a guy put it? "I'm not taking it out and—" Shadows, I couldn't even say it. "I'm not even sure I can stand." Maybe if I pointed out that I was weak from Talon's *feeding* Rider would take pity on me.

Except I had no idea what "take pity on me" looked like. Send me back to my room? If I couldn't walk how the hell could I get there?

"This is my fault, I can finish you off," Talon offered, drawing closer to me.

"No! I'm not— I can't— I—"

Oh Father, yes yes yes.

No!

“Not appropriate!” Rider snarled, the sound more animal than human... or rather fae. He yanked his blade from Talon’s shoulder and shoved him toward the Tower. “He’s human and barely a man. Leave before I stab you again.”

“Ah... right.” Talon looked stunned for a second as if he couldn’t believe what he’d just offered then shot me another apologetic look and ran back to the Tower.

“If you want to press charges against him, I’ll support you,” Rider said, his tone dark, his gaze locked on Talon. “It’s well within your right even though you’re no longer a lord. He’s a captain so I won’t be the judge. It has to go to the human-fae council in the Gold Tower. You’ll be assured a fair hearing.”

“I could press charges?” I had no idea I had those kind of rights. I’d never had those kind of rights before. But of course now I *could* press charges against Talon because they thought I was a man. If they knew I was a woman they’d probably laugh and shrug it off—

Except maybe not. The fae seemed to look at women differently than humans. Attacking a woman might be even worse in their culture than attacking a man.

“He shouldn’t have lost control like that.” Rider wiped his bloody dagger on his pant leg and shoved the weapon back into its sheath with more force than necessary.

His body was tight and I didn't need to see his face to tell he was furious. And while I could guess he was angry at Talon, I couldn't be sure that he also wasn't angry with me.

"I have no clue why he lost control like that. I've never seen his shadow do that before." He jerked a dark glare to me, his eyes narrowed, studying me, making the cold and need inside me swell. "His magic is darkness, so no one else knows that there's actually an entity inside him."

And really, if people did know, they'd be terrified of him. They'd probably lock him up, not caring that the shadow wasn't evil.

"No one else would understand," I said. I was kind of surprised Rider wasn't afraid of Talon's shadow since Talon had indicated no one else had seen or experienced the same heartbreaking loneliness I had. "It was an accident."

I knew that in my heart. His shadow had been starving and desperate and I had what it needed. I didn't know why it hadn't gone after Rider or why Talon hadn't been feeding it properly, but it hadn't meant to hurt me. That, and even if I did want to press charges, that would just draw more attention to me.

Movement drew my gaze to the pasture gate as the other novices, along with Lord Quill, jogged into the pasture and headed our way.

My attention locked on Quill's golden hair,

somehow catching sunlight that wasn't shining anywhere else in the Gray, and my pulse stuttered like it always did when I saw him. Except now my need was so much stronger than before, fueled by Talon's magic.

Crap. I had to get a hold of myself. I couldn't let the other novices see me making eyes at Lord Quill or Lord Rider for that matter. Without a doubt that would just be another thing they could use against me.

If they didn't give me trouble for being attracted to men — something that humans were taught was disgusting — then they'd accuse me of trying to get special attention, whether I was given special attention or not.

And as much as I wanted to run — or rather stagger — back to my room, wrap myself in all the blankets I had, and make myself come again, the others would see getting out of today's training as special attention.

I heaved myself to my feet, sending a wave of dizziness sweeping over me, and staggered to the closest boulder marking the running trail to keep my balance.

"Sit back down," Rider commanded.

"I'm all right. I just need a moment and then I need to get into the brushes so I can—" Another, stronger, wave of dizziness crashed over me.

"You've just gone white as a sheet. Sit down before you pass out and crack your skull open."

"I'm—"

"Sit." He grabbed the front of my jerkin, heaved me forward, making need blaze through me and the world lurch. Then he kicked my feet out from under me, and sat me back on the ground. "If you can't stand by the time they've run the trail, I'm sending you back to your room."

"What happened to running into the bushes to jerk off?" I groaned, the words slipping out before I could stop them.

"That was before you looked like you were going to puke and pass out... ah fuck," he swore. "He said you tasted like a fae. He must have fed on you like you were fae. Quill!"

Lord Quill's attention jumped to us, and he dropped the bag he'd been carrying and broke out into a full run.

"What's wrong?" He crouched in front of me and captured my chin, sending that shock of something I always felt when I made even the briefest of contact with Lord Quill zing through me.

I bit back a groan, determined to not fall in his emerald gaze like I had when I'd first met him in Herstind March. But with firm fingers, he forced me to raise my head to meet his eyes, and when I tried to squeeze my eyes shut, he forced my lids open and stared at me, making my body ache with need.

Oh Father! They were going to be the end of me. I

wanted him, Talon, Fantasy Man, even Lord Rider so badly. Now now now.

"Head injury?" Lord Quill turned my head, abruptly releasing me from his gaze and looking for blood while I strained against his grip to look back at him and maintain eye contact. I couldn't look away, I needed him to—

I reached to cup his cheeks, the urge to kiss him, take pleasure from him, was overwhelming.

No. Stop. Just stop. I wrenched my hands back and an all-too-feminine whimper escaped my lips, sending a feminine blush of embarrassment burning over my face.

Shit shit shit. I squeezed my eyes shut. "Please stop touching me."

"Talon injury," Rider replied, his voice grim.

Quill jerked his hand away. "Shit. But he dealt with it last night."

"Apparently not, and his allure seems to have a stronger affect on the boy than others," Lord Rider said.

The footsteps of the other novices drew closer, but I kept my eyes shut. I was already on the ground looking weak. I wasn't going to let them see my need for Lord Quill and Lord Rider, too.

"Looks like *his lordship* tripped," someone whispered, drawing snickers from the group.

"What an idiot," someone else whispered back.

"Two times around the trail. Now!" Rider barked. "Last one has to run it again with this bag of rocks after training is done."

The snickers stopped and their footsteps pounded away.

"I have to run too."

I rolled forward onto my hands and knees so I could stand, but Lord Rider grabbed the back of my jerkin and yanked me off the ground as if I didn't weigh anything.

I tried to glare at him, but that only made me more aware of how ruggedly beautiful he was. "They'll accuse me of getting special treatment."

"Talon just attacked you and I doubt you can stand let alone run or fight. You *are* getting special treatment." He shoved me into Quill's arms. "Get him to his room. You're excused from training this afternoon as well as your half shift of stable duty after the evening meal. I don't want to see you or hear of you leaving your room until the morning meal. Someone will bring you dinner."

CHAPTER 16
Rider

Quill tightened his grip on Sawyer, and the boy shuddered and released a strangled groan. Bright red spots of embarrassment stained his too-pale cheeks and colored his ears redder than his hair even as he tried to suck in breaths to get himself under control.

I bit back a growl. He was a mess, and I wanted to storm to the infirmary and stab Talon again.

I hadn't realized how strongly his allure affected Sawyer. I'd never seen the shadow's magic affect anyone, man or woman, like that before, and I sure as hell had never seen Talon's shadow explode from his body like that — and I'd been there when he'd gotten infected with the thing.

It had been like he hadn't even been in control, like the shadow had completely taken over, which either meant there was something going on with the shadow or there was something different about Sawyer Herstind.

I ran my hands through my hair and realized I'd pulled out most of my topknot. Swell. Sawyer was a mess. Talon was a mess. And I was getting awfully close to being a mess.

"Check on Talon in the infirmary on your way back," I said.

Quill gave me a tight nod. He adjusted the boy in his arms as if he were a damsel in distress and didn't bother to let him try walking with assistance, reminding me that the boy's torso was still terribly bruised.

Sawyer released another strangled groan, his body shaking with Talon's magic. "This is humiliating. I can walk."

"No," Quill said as he marched away. "You can't."

What a fucking disaster. I was going to kill Talon for losing control like that and — fuck! — Kit and Payne were going to kill *me* when they heard what had happened, and being the Lord Commander of the Black Guard wouldn't stop them. It hadn't before. It wouldn't now.

Kit was my cousin and had always been open with me. In fact, I invited it since he had the same kind of common sense Quill and Ash and usually Talon had. The only thing being the Lord Commander had gotten me was that now they told me off in private.

And even if Kit and Payne didn't know the truth about what had really happened — because the only other person beside me, Quill, and Ash who knew about Talon's shadow was Flint — they'd still think, like everyone, that Sawyer had been hurt, and I'd been somehow responsible... which I was. I didn't know how I could have stopped Talon from attacking Sawyer, but I should have thought of something.

As it was, both Kit and his mate liked the boy, and they were going to tear into me over it. He was shy and thoughtful — despite what the rest of the men thought — and it was obvious from their report after the evening meal last night that they were already feeling protective of him.

It had hurt to change them to an evening hunting shift knowing it meant I was taking away the only friends Sawyer had made so far, but I couldn't risk the safety of the Gray for one boy's feelings.

Except Talon had just made everything worse for him. Missing this afternoon's training— hell, being seen on his ass on the ground by the other novices would perpetuate their belief that Sawyer was soft and spoiled. And by sending him to his room and having someone bring him dinner that belief would only get stronger.

But there was no way he'd have been able to run and fight, let alone move. And Quill had to have agreed because he'd carried the boy away.

The first of the novices came down the hill and raced back up the other one for their second pass around the trail, and I undid the leather tie no longer keeping my hair out of my eyes and retied my topknot, trying to physically as well as emotionally pull my shit back together.

I'd wanted Talon to help me with the advanced novices for the rest of the rotation and into the next one before he had to return to the Gold Tower to check in, but now I wasn't sure.

He'd said his shadow was fine and wouldn't need to feed again anytime soon, which meant the power of his allure should be weaker than before, but would either him or Sawyer be able to concentrate if they were working together? Hell, would they even be able to concentrate if they were within sight of each other?

Damn it. He'd said he'd dealt with it.

I punched the boulder beside me with enough force to split open my first two knuckles with a satisfying bite of pain and break away a large chunk of stone. I needed to run, let my wolf out, and kill shadows. If I wasn't being haunted by a stunning redhead every time I closed my eyes, I'd have been able to deal with Talon and Sawyer.

But that was just an excuse. I should have been able to focus despite my thoughts being captured by Sage and the turmoil I felt about her. I couldn't stop thinking about her and yet I *did not* — no way in hell did I — want another mate.

Except it had been two days and I still felt guilty about refusing to show her the Garden. Which didn't make any sense. Turning down the few women who'd approached me since I'd become eligible to be a mate had never bothered me before.

Why this one? Why now?

Because she reminded me of Isemay and I was coming up on the anniversary of her passing. Isemay had been soft and shy and guarded like Sage with a spark that had burned brighter than any human or fae I'd ever met. Sage made me lonely for what I'd lost. That was all.

And not at all what I should be focusing on.

The first of the novices, a group of three fae, ran off the trail, huffing with exertion. They were my best fighters in this year's group of novices and the fastest runners, and with another hunting team out of commission, I was tempted to put them straight into the rotation and not bother with the rest of the novice training for them.

Talon had wholeheartedly agreed with that plan, Ash had said they weren't any of the novices he was concerned about, while Quill, ever the voice of reason, had wanted to wait and see how they handled this rotation before making his decision.

Two more fae with Mikel and Durand on their

heels raced between the boulders marking the trail then the rest of the fae, Ambrose, and Hamelin followed. Bramwell, who was big, but not as slow as I'd expect for a human his size, followed a few minutes later along with the rest of the novices we were going to put into advanced training.

I studied them, trying to figure out which one of them was Ash... because one of them had to be Ash.

Sawyer was the biggest target among the novices, and if Ash was disguised as a weaker novice, he'd usually be convincing the others to support the boy. But it didn't look like anyone was even thinking about stepping up to befriend Sawyer which meant Ash was one of the stronger novices and was likely trying to worm his way in with the potential troublemakers to keep an eye on them.

Which was bad luck for Sawyer. Having a few other novices befriending him early on would go a long way to convincing the other Guardsmen to accept him.

The rest of the novices finished their run and the poor chef's assistant, a heavy-set young man who'd probably never run a day in his life, came in last.

"Tyon," I said to him. "After training, once around the trail with the rocks." I didn't particularly like this part of the training, but it was an effective way to quickly strengthen the weakest novices.

His gaze swept over the group and he frowned. "What about Sawyer?"

"Sawyer's on bedrest for the rest of the day," I said.

A flurry of murmurs swept through the group and Mikel huffed. "Coddling him will only get the rest of us killed."

No shit. But I wasn't coddling him, and it wasn't Mikel's place to tell me how to deal with my men even if I was. His snarky remarks, especially regarding how I was handling things needed to be stopped and now.

"Congratulations, novice," I told him. "You get to run the trail with Tyon at the end of today's training with the other bag of rocks." I strode toward the fighting circles scraped into the rocky ground.

"Doesn't make what I said any less untrue," Mikel shot back, making me bristle.

"Know your place!" I snapped, letting my wolf darken my tone.

Mikel's eyes widened and he paled.

Yes, I was known to be less strict than other military commanders in the human and fae realms, and I had no doubt Mikel's friends and family who'd preceded him here had told him that. We needed a brotherhood in the Black Tower as much as we needed a fighting force, and I was willing to allow a certain amount of leeway among my men to encourage that, but I was still in charge and it looked like this novice needed to be reminded of that.

"Two times around the trail," I snarled, my wolf fighting to take over completely. "I shouldn't have to remind you. I'm the Lord Commander. You will show me the respect I've earned, or did your family not teach you any of that?"

Mikel straightened and raised his chin. "Yes, my lord."

"We're wrestling today," I announced as Quill rejoined me.

He glanced at the bag of practice daggers that he'd brought down from the storage locker in the indoor practice hall but kept a straight face at the sudden change of plans.

Except everyone else looked at the bag as well. They'd probably been told by the other Guardsmen at the midday meal that they were going to be tested and training in daggers this afternoon, and me changing my plans just confirmed that I was coddling Sawyer. Except with his slight stature, there was no point in testing his wrestling abilities. Even if he had some skill, he was going to get pummeled and that wouldn't be helpful for anyone.

"Wrestling," I repeated.

"He's changed his mind because the runt isn't here," Durand whispered out of the corner of his mouth, barely loud enough for me to hear — and I wouldn't have been able to hear it if I hadn't been a shifter.

He stood at the back of the group with Hamelin, Bramwell, and Ambrose and all four of them shared knowing looks as if they'd come to a conclusion, one I had no doubt involved Sawyer and my seeming inability to treat him like everyone else.

Fuck. I had enough to handle with Talon losing control and Sawyer being almost incapacitated.

Why couldn't the boy have just come through the ring before dark? None of this would be a problem if he'd just followed proper protocol.

Except even if he had, I suspected the others would still look down on him. He was a nobleman and so damned small. No one wanted to fight shadows with him because he looked weak, and if it didn't look like I was trying to turn him into a proper Guardsman then they were going to do it themselves. Their lives depended on Sawyer's ability to fight.

And while I couldn't blame their line of thinking, I couldn't allow them to take Sawyer's training into their own hands.

I didn't think the boy was fragile. In fact, him trying to get up and run after Talon had attacked him just proved he was too stubborn for his own good, but I also was far too aware of how easily human's bodies and minds broke.

Too much *help* from Mikel and his friends could prove Talon's fears true, and if Sawyer didn't outright kill himself, he'd still be a useless mess that would take even more time and energy to fix to turn him into a Guardsmen.

"Tyon!" I snapped making the poor man jerk to attention and squeak with fright. "Thank Durand. He just volunteered to do your lap around the trail with the bag of rocks."

"Thank you, my lord," Tyon stammered.

I swept my glare over the novices, my wolf curling my lips back in a sneer, making all the fae stiffen.

They knew my beast was what had made me one of the deadliest hunters in the Guard before I'd been promoted to Lord Commander, and while I had extraordinary patience for a fae with an animal form, part of my nature was still a predator.

And Goddess help me, I was barely holding on.

A few more pushes and my claws would come out. I didn't need disrespect from the novices and I sure as hell didn't need Talon losing control. It was a miracle that Sawyer hadn't decided to press charges. Except that was just more proof that he wasn't the haughty noble they thought he was.

"Next man who speaks out of turn is tossed out of novice training and on stable duty all day every day until I'm no longer angry, and I'm a wolf," I snarled, my fingers extending into claws and my wolf straining against my control. "My regular state of mind is angry."

"Has the Lord Commander made himself clear?" Quill called out, his expression as dark and hard as mine, backing me up even though he was far more even-tempered that I was.

The novices straightened. “Yes, my lord.”

“Good. Now Rue—” I barked, making the fae’s eyes widen with fear. “You and Quill demonstrate the basics of wrestling techniques.” He breathed a sigh of relief to know he wasn’t going to be wrestling me or my wolf while I was riled up.

I crossed my arms and glared at them as Quill started the lesson. My wolf snarled inside me. It wanted to tear something to pieces, but I had to get through this lesson first. I could only pray that Sawyer would be recovered from Talon’s feeding tomorrow morning, because if he hadn’t and I was forced to keep him in bed, keeping the other novices from taking his training into their own hands was going to become more difficult. And now that I’d pulled rank on them, I doubted they were going to let me see it.

Fuck. If Ash hadn’t befriended the troublemakers yet, he needed to do so now, because the way things were going, the situation could get out of hand quickly.

CHAPTER 17

Quill

THE BELL for the early shift's evening meal rang. Rider barked a harsh command to Mikel and Duran to pick up their bags of rocks and start running, then growled at Rue to grab the bag of practice daggers and take them back to the indoor practice hall.

With a huff, he gruffly dismissed the rest of the novices who hurried back to the Tower, moving quickly despite the afternoon's strenuous lesson as if they were afraid Rider might change his mind and extend the day's training.

And rightly so. He'd been hard on them and his wolf was still barely under control.

It was a miracle he'd just stood by and didn't fight one of the fae — or me — in an attempt to vent his anger and regain control. And yet despite the hours the lesson had taken, he still looked like he needed a fight. Which only spoke to how pissed off he was over the whole Talon-Sawyer situation.

"So what happened?" I asked, keeping my attention on our surroundings, ensuring there wasn't anyone within earshot.

This wasn't a conversation I or Rider wanted anyone else to hear, but I also didn't want to wait until we'd climbed the stairs to either of our suites at the top of the Tower.

Sawyer had been a shivering, whimpering mess when I'd set him on his bed, looking more like the child Talon thought him to be than the man the humans claimed.

I'd never seen Talon's magic do that to someone before. Sure, when the shadow had been particularly hungry, some of the women attending the court at the Gold Tower had thrown themselves at Talon, but they hadn't desired anyone else — like Sawyer seemed to be with me — and they hadn't been on the verge of passing out after Talon had given in to his shadow's hunger.

"I have no fucking idea," Rider snarled, not needing more of an explanation to know what I was talking about. "Talon came off the trail, his shadow shot out of him, and just attacked the boy. You're closest with him. Has his shadow ever done that before?"

"Not that he's told me."

This was bad. If the shadow was getting more aggressive, it was going to be harder to keep it a secret. That realization must have scared Talon and he'd yanked it back before it had properly fed. It was the only explanation why Sawyer had still been a wreck when I'd carried him to his room.

"He should have just let it feed," I said, "not left Sawyer hanging."

Even barely knowing Sawyer, that would have embarrassed him. But better a mess in his pants than his current state of suffering.

"He did," Rider said, unbuckling his sword belt and shoving it — along with his sheathed sword and three long daggers — into my hands.

"But Sawyer—"

"Was still fucked up on Talon's allure? Yeah. It's a problem. Just like the other novices getting it in their heads to take Sawyer's training into their own hands."

He shrugged out of his jerkin and added it to the pile in my arms, the heavy fabric made heavier by the extra daggers attached to it.

"I need to hunt before I kill someone," he said. "Take a meal to the boy and check on Talon. If I'm not in the Garden when it's time to meet Ash, tell him he better be best friends with Mikel and his gang or close to the boy by the end of tomorrow because Talon just painted a target on his back, and I can't properly discipline anyone until they've done something."

He yanked his shirt off over his head, revealing the thin white scars that streaked across his bulky chest, partially hidden by a dusting of dark hair. They were a testament to how many shadows he'd fought and survived during his time in the Guard.

With a growl, he pulled off his boots and shucked his pants, leaving them in a pile at my feet, and then, with stomach-churning bone crunching, he shifted into his massive black wolf.

I shuddered, grateful I wasn't a shifter. As much as I'd do almost anything for magic, I would rather it be anything other than the ability to change into an animal. Rider had confessed one drunken night before we'd seen our first half century that shifting was excruciating and it didn't matter which way he shifted, beast to man or man to beast, it hurt either way.

He huffed at me, his breath hitting me in the chest, then bounded away. Given how he'd practically been vibrating trying to control his wolf during the training session, I doubted we'd see him in the Garden. He'd probably meet up with Kit and Payne and join their hunt.

At least I hoped he did. Even turning into a vicious creature easily twice the size of a regular wolf didn't mean he could win every fight against every shadow he came across while alone.

The question now was if he had enough control over his primal nature to think that clearly.

I gathered the rest of Rider's clothing, marched back to the Black Tower, and climbed the stairs to the top of the main tower to Rider's suite where I set his clothes on the couch in his sitting room.

His room was identical to the rooms Talon and I had been assigned, as well as the guest suite — the only other suite on this level. That room should have been Ash's when he wasn't undercover, but he'd refused it, keeping his small, single suite in the Tower's left wing instead.

Each room had a private bathing room, a bedroom, a sitting room, and shared a balcony with the room beside it, but if I hadn't known this was Rider's room, I'd never have been able to figure it out.

With the exception of a weapons rack filled with a variety of weapons all showing signs of use, there was nothing personal in his sitting room, as if he'd never fully moved into the position of Lord Commander even though he'd held the job for forty-three years.

Even Talon and I had added a few personal touches to our suites, and we only used the suites when we were in the Gray training novices or for special meetings. Our primary residences were in our respective Towers, me in the White Tower and Talon in the Gold.

I stepped back into the hall. The top floor of the

Black Tower's central tower was an unusual design with a large hole in the center — protected by a waist-high railing — that allowed the light from the skylight above to shine down to the library below. The skylight feature didn't add as much light in the Black Tower as it did in the White Tower because the sun hardly ever broke through the clouds and mist in the Gray, but it did help alleviate some of the oppressive darkness in the library, something the human Guardsmen probably didn't notice but the fae Guardsmen did.

Across the opening lay the doors to my suite and Talon's. For a moment I contemplated checking in on him since I'd already climbed all the stairs, but making sure Sawyer was all right and had something to eat was my first priority.

Talon was probably worried and angry at himself for losing control, but he'd survive. He, at least, hadn't been banished to his room and could go down to the kitchen to get something if he was hungry. Sawyer couldn't. That, and Sawyer was in complete shock. I wasn't sure, even if he wanted to and had permission, if he'd be able to make it to the kitchen.

Not to mention, if I asked Talon, he'd tell me to check on Sawyer first. He was probably worried out of his mind that he'd seriously and permanently hurt the boy. And as much as Talon displayed a fun-loving, relaxed persona, he felt everything — love, joy, heartache, worry — deeply, and he'd be upset if I didn't have an update on Sawyer's condition.

With that decided, I grabbed a large evening meal from the kitchen and took it to Sawyer's room. I didn't know how hungry he'd be. From his shivering, pale complexion, and unfocused eyes, he looked like he'd been drained deeply, more deeply than the shadow had drained anyone before.

Except he'd still been under the influence of Talon's allure which suggested the shadow hadn't actually drained him.

Regardless, if he'd been drained of vitality, he'd be hungry. If he hadn't been, and if the allure was still raging through his system, he'd be hungry for something else.

If he asked, would I give him what he desired? He wasn't fae and he wasn't who I wanted... because I wanted his sister.

Having sex with him, even if it was just sucking him off, could affect whatever working relationship we needed to have. Humans didn't see sex the same way fae did and they certainly didn't see sex between men the same way at all.

Talon had been almost certain the boy hadn't fully realized he was attracted to other men until he'd stumbled across him the other night in the bathhouse and that was something many humans struggled to come to terms with.

No, given what I'd observed from Sawyer over the last couple of days, he wouldn't ask anything of me no matter how much Talon's allure was raging through him.

Which then begged the question, would I push the issue? Could I let him suffer for the rest of the night or — hell! I had no idea how long he'd suffer. Could I let him suffer when I could release the need I knew was thrumming through him?

Talon's magic had never affected anyone like this before, and I had no doubt Talon and Rider were wondering what was different. Was it something to do with Talon's shadow or something to do with Sawyer Herstind.

And if it was something to do with Sawyer, did that also mean his sister was special? Would that explain why I couldn't stop thinking of her, why every time I closed my eyes, I saw her staring at me, her brown gaze shocked and filled with terror.

Goddess, half the time I looked at Sawyer I saw her. Even coming out of the Tower at the beginning of this afternoon's training, I'd thought for a heart-stopping moment that it had been Sawyer's sister sitting on the ground in front of Rider.

My pulse irrationally picked up at the thought of her. Sawyer had said she was safe, but was she? The human realm was dangerous for women. They had no say in their lives. The only women I'd come across who had any say, sold their bodies and even then not all pleasure houses let their women be as independent as the pleasure house in Lehyrst that the Guard frequented.

I gritted my teeth against the urge to demand he tell me where his sister was so I could take her to safety and knocked on his door.

It's only a fascination. The feelings aren't real. I'd never experienced a soul bond before — and without any magic the chances of being bound to a woman were slim to none — so I couldn't possibly think that what I felt for Sawyer's sister was a bond.

But Goddess it felt like one.

Hope and need and aching desperation flooded me. Somehow I had to convince Sawyer to tell me where she was so I could get her, at the very least, into the fae realm. She still wouldn't be a full citizen like our women, but at least she'd be treated with more respect.

Jeez. Talon wasn't the only one losing control.

But maybe if I got her to safety that would ease my mind. Maybe that was all I needed to do and I'd be able to stop thinking about her.

I knocked again. "Sawyer, it's Quill. I've brought your evening meal."

"Just set it outside," he said, his voice barely audible and strained.

Crap. That didn't sound good at all. "I need to know you're all right."

"I'm all right," he called back. "Please. Just leave it."

Something thudded on the other side of the door. It didn't sound heavy enough to be a body... but his body was rather small... "Sawyer? I'm coming in."

CHAPTER 18

I OPENED the door and Sawyer sagged onto the edge of his bed, shivering uncontrollably, his complexion shockingly pale.

"You're not all right." I set the tray on the chest at the foot of the narrow bed. "I'm going to get Flint."

"Don't," he gasped as I turned to leave. "I'm better than before. A meal and a good night's sleep is all I need. There's no point in bothering the healer."

He lurched forward and grasped my sleeve to stop me, and I caught his arm, steadying him before he collapsed and hit the floor.

A shock of something zinged through my hand and my vision wavered, turning him into his sister, just like how she'd been when I'd said his name in Herstind castle. Then he sagged back onto his bed and my vision cleared.

"Would the healer even know what to do with me?" he asked, his voice small. "Does he know about Talon's... magic?"

"That it's... special?" I asked, trying to figure out how much Talon and Rider might have let slip to Sawyer or how much he might have figured out about the nature of Talon's magic.

"Yes," Sawyer replied, not giving me much more of a clue about what he did or didn't know than his hesitation before magic had.

"Flint knows." But he probably wouldn't know what to do with Sawyer. Flint's healing magic specialized in the body, not a person's soul or spark, and our best guess was that Talon's shadow consumed something to do with soul or spark. With the exception of making someone a little tired and maybe a bit chilly, the shadow didn't affect the physical body.

Except Sawyer looked ready to pass out, was far too pale, and couldn't stop shivering despite still being dressed in his shirt and pants.

"Can we wait until morning? It's bad enough I was excused from training," he said through chattering teeth. "If the healer comes running, I'll look even more spoiled and selfish."

Or less. If Flint checked him out then at least it would look like we had good reason to put him on bedrest for the rest of the day. Of course, if he was fine by morning then the other Guardsmen could construe

Flint rushing to Sawyer's room as giving the boy special attention.

"Have you at least been able to deal with the effect of Talon's allure?" I asked, helping him prop himself up against the wall at the head of his bed so he could eat.

"I have," he replied, his breathy voice belying his words.

"Let me see." I leaned forward to look in his eyes and check his pupils.

He raised his gaze, and again, for a too-fast pounding of my heart, I saw his sister, those same brown eyes with a hint of emerald as if my mind really wanted her— *him* to be fae instead of human.

He trembled and his breath picked up, but he managed to meet my gaze. I could still sense his arousal, see it in the tension in his body, but his pupils had returned to normal and weren't fully covering his irises like they had been before, and he didn't seem as desperate as he'd been when I'd carried him from the training grounds.

"All right. We'll wait until morning."

I grabbed the blankets — he had both the summer and winter ones he'd been assigned on his bed even though it was still summer — and drew them over his body, noticing that he wore the pants he'd ripped the other day. The tear had been so finely stitched it was only noticeable because I was so close.

"Did you stitch that tear yourself?" I asked.

"Yeah." He dropped his gaze and pulled the blankets up his body almost to his chin. "Lord Rider said I wouldn't get new pants so I asked the quartermaster for a needle and thread."

"You're going to want to show him that." I grabbed the tray with his food and set it on the narrow bed between us, making his eyes widen in surprise.

"How much do you think I eat?" he asked. "You're not going to be like Payne who thinks giving me more food is going to make me grow faster. I'm not going to be able to eat all of this."

"I didn't know how hungry you'd be." I picked up one of the slices of warm, buttered bread and took a bite. "The effects of Talon's magic can make you hungry." At least — thank the Goddess! — he wasn't still desperate for a sexual release and I didn't have to decide if I was going to help him with that or not.

"Not your first time dealing with one of his... donors?" he asked, dipping his spoon into his stew. But when he tried to raise it to his mouth he was shaking so hard there wasn't much left on the utensil by the time it reached his lips.

"Here, let me help." I started to move but he tensed, freezing like a small animal caught in Rider's sights.

"I've got it." He cupped the bowl between his small hands and raised it to his lips, slurping his dinner.

I took another bite of my bread. Did he fear that I'd take advantage of him, or was he just so stubborn he wouldn't accept help eating when he clearly was too shaky and weak to do it by himself. Even now, the bowl trembled against his lips as if the effort to hold it up was too much for him.

He took another big gulp, bigger than he should have, swallowed and set the bowl back down, gasping for breath. Jeez. It was like he'd already taken lessons from Rider on extreme stubbornness. Except I had a feeling if I told Sawyer that it was all right to ask for help, he'd just nod and ignore me like Rider always did.

Which meant the only thing I could do for him was to be a friend, someone he could trust when things got too difficult for him and he finally reached the end of his rope — which given how stubborn he was would mean that things were completely out of hand and dire.

Rider had to be his commander and he didn't do *feelings* very well, Talon probably terrified him now, and he didn't even know Ash existed. That, and given that none of the novices had tried to befriend Sawyer, Ash was probably one of the other eight human novices we were going to put in the advanced training.

And while Talon had said Sawyer had become friends with Kit, Payne, and Lewin, they were back on a proper hunting shift and would be harder to get a hold of if Sawyer needed help.

Which meant it was up to me to take Talon's place

fostering a relationship with Sawyer, at least until I had to return to my duties at the White Tower.

"You really should show the quartermaster your work," I said, changing the topic. I was still worried, but pushing him about his condition wouldn't get me anywhere. "With that kind of skill he's going to want you mending all our clothes. You'll never have to muck another stall again."

"Not sure how the other Guardsmen will take that," he replied, then took another big gulp of stew.

"Many would say sewing for the quartermaster is a harder job than mucking stables." I nudged a piece of buttered bread closer to his hand and he picked it up and took a bite. "Payne certainly would. When he first got here he accidentally sewed three sets of pantlegs together before the quartermaster noticed."

"How could he not know he was sewing pantlegs together?" Sawyer asked as he ripped off another chunk of bread and popped it in his mouth, his lips turned up in a half smile that eased some of the tension in my chest.

"I have no idea," I chuckled. "He's far from dumb. I don't think he'd ever sewn anything in his life before. He's lucky enough to have two older sisters and one of them makes the most amazing dresses."

Sawyer's eyes widened. "Two? That's rare isn't it?"

"It is," I replied. "I'm surprised you know that."

Sawyer dropped his gaze, suddenly shy and uncomfortable with me again. “I asked Kit, Payne, and Lewin a little about fae culture before their shift was changed. I figured if half the men I’m going to— ah... spend the rest of my life with are fae, I should probably know more about you— I mean your people.”

Which was smart thinking. Most of the problems between fae and human novices came because of a lack of understanding of each other’s culture. “I’m happy to answer any questions you might have, and I have no doubt once your schedule realigns with Kit and Payne’s again, they’ll be happy to as well.”

He nodded, his gaze still on his shaking hands as he ripped another chunk from the bread. “I think my biggest problem is that I don’t know what I don’t know. I’m not even sure what to ask about.”

“Well what did you ask Kit and Payne?”

“About women—”

“You did, did you?” I chuckled, a hint of teasing slipping into my tone.

“I mean— I, ah... I know I’m fae-touched but—” His ears turned bright red, but I didn’t know if it was embarrassment over talking about women or admitting he was also sexually attracted to men, so I took a guess—

“Just because you’re attracted to men, doesn’t mean you can’t also be attracted to women,” I reassured.

He bobbed his head and shoved the piece of bread into his mouth.

"There's nothing wrong with you for desiring what you desire and no one here will think worse of you for it." And if they did, Payne would probably pummel them.

"No, they have other reasons to think badly of me," he huffed. "And rightly so. I honestly didn't know I shouldn't have gone through the ring after dark."

Which was his biggest problem. The other Guardsmen might have been concerned about him because he was a nobleman's son, but they would have just been concerned about him being lazy and selfish if he hadn't screwed up so badly just by arriving.

And Talon had just made everything worse for him. If Sawyer had managed to keep his head down for a couple of rotations, the men would have forgiven him for his mistake and grudgingly welcomed him into the brotherhood, because Sawyer didn't seem selfish at all.

But now, because we'd taken him out of training only three days after arriving, we'd just added to their fears that he was going to be a problem.

And there wasn't anything I could do about that right now so...

"Why were you asking them about our women?" I asked, trying to lighten the mood again. "Hoping they're just as pretty as Talon?" I quipped.

"He is rather... striking."

Sawyer's blush swept from his ears across his forehead and cheeks and down his neck, making me groan inwardly at my mistake. I shouldn't have reminded him of his attraction to Talon, not if there was any trace of Talon's allure still in his system.

"But no... yes? I overheard some of the fae talking about this Garden and about a new arrival, and Payne had mentioned something about not being eligible for a female mate, and all of that seemed... strange," he said in a rush.

"It probably is strange to you," I said. "The first time I visited your realm I'd been shocked at how many women there were. They were everywhere."

I'd been young, just old enough to be in the Garden, and couldn't believe my eyes at all the women and children. Then I couldn't believe my eyes at how many of them were treated... which made me think of his sister.

My pulse picked up and I fought to hide the sudden fear racing through me. I couldn't lose it on him like I had the other day when I'd learned that their step-father hit both him and his sister. He'd just panic again and clam up and for the sake of my sanity, I couldn't have that happen.

"We treat our women differently, too. Your sister has lost whatever prospects she might have had running away with you," I said carefully.

"Her *prospects,*" he replied, making prospects sound

like a dirty word, "weren't good or wanted. She's better off no longer being a nobleman's daughter."

"But now what? Her options are limited in your realm."

"She'll be all right." He grabbed his bowl of stew and took another big slurp, keeping his gaze down. I could practically see his emotional walls coming up again.

"She could be better than all right," I pressed. "I could arrange for her to live in my realm." Goddess I needed her to be in my realm and safe. "If she can read, I can probably get her a position as an assistant or novice scribe at the White Tower."

Sawyer's gaze jerked up to me and again — Goddess be damned again! — I saw *her* instead of him. "For what price? You don't know me and you don't know her. What do you want with her?"

"Nothing. I—" How could I explain to him that I was obsessing over his sister?

No. I couldn't. No brother wanted to hear that a strange man couldn't stop thinking about his sister. He was going to think I wanted to have sex with her—

Did I want to have sex with her?

Yes!

No?

I had no clue. I just had to know she was safe.

"She's safe where she is," he replied, his voice soft,

except I could hear his unspoken "for now" hanging in the silence as he dropped his gaze again.

"She's not if she's alone."

"She's not alone." He took another slurp of his stew, the quivering in his hands increasing. "She just needs to be patient for a few weeks and then everything will be fine."

Except the word *fine* came out strained, twisting my worry for her tighter.

"But if I take her to my realm, she won't have to settle for fine." I leaned forward and grabbed his wrists, stopping him from hiding behind his stew bowl. "Just tell me where she is."

"She's fine." He trembled in my grip, his skin shockingly cold. "Everything will be fine."

Except it sounded like he was trying to convince himself of that.

"I'm tired," he said, his gaze locked on my hands around his wrists. "May I rest?"

I opened my mouth to order him to tell me where his sister was, but managed to snap it shut before saying anything.

What the hell was wrong with me?

She wasn't my destined mate. She couldn't be. She was human. I had to stop thinking about her. That, and I'd already figured out Sawyer was stubborn like Rider which meant even if I did command him to tell me her location, he wouldn't.

No, I needed to be patient. I could get him to tell me the truth, I just needed to be smart about it and win his trust first, not to mention figure out how to stop obsessing about her.

CHAPTER 19
Talon

I PACED the sitting room of my suite, stomping between the wooden door leading to the balcony and the large table on the other side of the room that was covered with reports along with my jerkin and sword belt.

My mind whirled and my shoulder throbbed where Rider had stabbed me. Flint had stitched me up and added enough magic to speed up my natural healing but hadn't done much more, saving his magic in the event other Guardsmen ran into real trouble while on patrol.

I jerked away from the table back toward the door, rubbing my face as if that would help me think straight.

I had no idea what had happened. My eyes had landed on Sawyer and my shadow had just exploded from my body, its hunger overwhelming and ferocious.

Goddess, it was still ferocious, writhing under my skin and straining to break free and take over again.

It twisted around the spark in the core of my being that let me control the shadows around me and strained to get back to Sawyer. It was still hungry for whatever it was that it consumed, and it had taken more from Sawyer than anyone before. It should have been satisfied.

I'd thought when I'd told Rider that it was satisfied that it had been.

But really it had just been shocked and scared. Just like I'd been.

It had desired Sawyer from the moment it had sensed him in the bathing room beneath the barracks, and its hunger had only grown stronger each time our paths crossed.

Then I'd crested the final hill on the running trail and Sawyer's gaze had leaped to mine. I'd gone instantly hard, my cock straining against the front of my pants, and my shadow had jerked me forward and seized hold of the boy before I could even think of fighting it.

The sudden explosion of desire had shocked me... but it had also shocked my shadow and now both of us were confused as hell.

There was something about Sawyer Herstind that it craved, that made it ravenous, and we both knew if we didn't figure out how to control ourselves, we could kill the boy.

Goddess, we might have already permanently hurt him.

My shadow had never drained anyone so deeply, never left a person weak and shaking and yet still fully affected by its allure. The rush from Sawyer had been powerful and breathtaking and so strong neither of us had realized he'd actually come, and coming should have burned off all of my shadow's seductive magic from his body.

Except it hadn't. The boy had been desperate for more and, from the way he'd looked at Rider, he hadn't cared if his release had come from me or Rider, which was another thing that had never happened before.

And damn if I hadn't wanted to give him more. I'd wanted to wrap my hand around his cock, push my own cock into him, and make him see stars.

My cheeks heated with embarrassment. I couldn't believe I'd offered to make him come again. It had been highly inappropriate. And if Sawyer hadn't fully accepted that he was attracted to men, it was something that could make him withdraw further into his shell. I could only pray I hadn't done serious emotional or physical damage to him.

A sense of agreement and worry from my shadow swept through me. It didn't want to hurt Sawyer either and knew it needed to be more careful next time.

There might not be a next time, I thought at it even though we didn't communicate with words but with feelings and intentions.

It responded with a sense of certainty that there would be a next time. But not for a while. Not until Sawyer had recovered.

Except just thinking about Sawyer reminded it of its hunger and how delicious he'd tasted.

Someone knocked on my door. I prayed it was Quill with an update on Sawyer's condition, but feared it was Rider, ready to reprimand me for losing control.

With my stomach churning, I opened it.

Quill stood in the hall. Relief flickered in my chest, but it only lasted a moment. Quill's expression was tight with concern and my thoughts instantly jumped to Sawyer and the condition he'd been in when Rider had sent me to the infirmary.

Oh, Goddess. Had I permanently hurt him? Had I killed him?

"Is he all right?" I asked even as the urge to go to him swelled inside me.

"Shaken and drained," Quill said as he entered.

I forced myself to close the door and not check on Sawyer myself. I doubted he'd want to see me, especially if he hadn't managed to alleviate the rest of my shadow's allure.

That, and I didn't know if my shadow could contain its allure in Sawyer's presence yet. It was somehow still hungry, wanting me to drive into him and feed it properly with sex not just desire. Which meant I would still be radiating its allure whether either of us wanted it to or not.

Quill reached the middle of the room then glared at me still standing with my hand on the latch. "What happened?"

I heaved myself away from the door and sagged onto the nearby couch.

"I have no idea." And that was one of the things that terrified me. "The shadow just took over and fed off him like he was fae. He tastes like he's fae."

A shudder swept through me with a mix of satisfaction and hunger. Whatever the shadow craved, Sawyer had it in abundance, and I had no idea how long I, or my shadow, would be able to resist its urges.

Quill unbuckled his sword belt and set it on the table beside mine then eased onto the couch beside me. I shifted, putting my legs on either side of him, so I could wrap my arms around him and hold him against my chest, taking comfort in his body and praying his calm nature would help steady me and my shadow.

"But he's clearly human," Quill replied, leaning into me.

"Maybe his spark is strong." Except that didn't make sense because fae had stronger sparks than humans and my shadow had never reacted to them like it had Sawyer.

"Strong enough to taste like a fae?" Quill frowned. "Have you fed on a fae-touched human before? Maybe that's the difference."

"Once, but it wasn't anything like with Sawyer. The shadow wanted Sawyer— *still* wants him."

It churned within me, its allure radiating from my body and making Quill's eyes roll back even though it was Sawyer it really wanted.

Damn it. *You're fine. You've just had the biggest fucking meal you've ever had.*

"How is it still hungry?" Quill breathed.

Its allure surged stronger and Quill shivered, the movement of his body turning me instantly hard. Again. Fuck. I'd thought the shadow and I had come to an understanding. It wasn't evil. It was trapped inside me and it understood that we couldn't draw attention to ourselves.

"I've had a few days rest. I can give it another feeding," Quill said, his words slurred with his desire.

Stop it, I thought at it even as my hands slid down to the laces on Quill's pants. But a new emotion billowed within me in response.

It didn't really want to feed. It wanted... comfort. Something within Sawyer comforted it and Quill was willing to offer a little bit of that comfort as well.

Quill shifted, giving me better access down the front of his pants, the movement grinding his back against my cock and making my breath hitch.

Goddess be damned, *I* needed comfort as well.

"It really wants Sawyer again," I groaned, sliding my hand into Quill's pants.

"Sawyer—" he started.

I brushed my thumb over his tip, sliding through the precum already beaded there, and made his breath hitch.

My shadow shuddered with pleasure.

We loved that sound, loved the look of bliss on Quill's face, and hated how it broke my heart a little more each time we made love to him. Because if he was truly going to be mine, he'd have to abandon his dream of being mated to a woman.

"Sawyer can't take another feeding like that anytime soon," he said on a soft moan.

"The shadow agrees." It— *I* pushed my hand deeper in his pants and wrapped my fingers around the base of his cock. I wanted this as much as my shadow did, needed the comfort Quill was offering with his body. "What happened shocked it as much as it shocked the rest of us. It'll be more cautious next time."

"You honestly think Sawyer will let there be a next time?" he asked as I drew my hand up his length. "You have to ask permission for anything more. You can't just attack him again."

"I think he'll let it feed." I pressed my lips against his jaw and pumped my hand down, drawing another soft moan that made my shadow shiver with pleasure. "When the shadow overwhelmed him, he felt it like I do, felt its hunger and loneliness. But I doubt Rider will let it happen even if Sawyer agrees. And I shouldn't let it happen, either, no matter what my shadow wants. I could have seriously hurt the boy. I still might have."

And the shadow could have hurt more than just his body. For all I knew he was in the middle of a crisis, fully realizing that he desired men when all his life he'd probably been told women were the only ones he was supposed to desire.

"I thought I had everything under control," I murmured more to myself then Quill.

But my shadow had possessed me in a way he'd never possessed me before and I hadn't realized just how hungry he'd been... still was.

CHAPTER 20

Talon

"Hey." Quill rolled over to kneel between my thighs and capture me with his piercing emerald gaze. "We'll figure it out. We always do."

His sincerity filled me with love and longing. Rider had been there when the shadow had gotten caught up in my shadow magic and been trapped inside me and had helped me out as best he could, but Quill was the one who'd really nursed me back to sanity and helped me find my new balance.

If it hadn't been for him, I probably would have still been a sobbing mess, jumping at sensations and emotions that weren't mine, thinking I was losing my mind.

"Do you think any of the magisters at the White Tower have discovered anything more about shadows?" I asked.

We'd already gone through all the texts we could find and hadn't found a way to separate the shadow from my magic. But it had been years since we'd last checked.

The shadow's sour anger at being separated from me grew stronger and it sent a surge of seductive magic slamming into Quill.

Quill groaned and his breath picked up. He tugged at the laces on my pants, but they tangled and his sex drugged body and mind struggled to undo them.

"Here." I nudged his hands away and freed my cock, my flesh aching and hypersensitive.

His pupils swelled with my shadow's magic, fully devouring his green irises, and his tongue darted over his bottom lip, making my own desire — on top of my shadow's — burn hotter. With a sigh, he wrapped his fingers around me, dipped forward, and sucked me deep into his mouth.

My balls tightened, my cock already hard as hell, threatening to release, and I knew I needed to get him undressed and be buried inside him to give my shadow the deepest feeding it could get.

Rider needed me to help train the novices and I couldn't afford for it to attack Sawyer again. But despite knowing that, I still grabbed a fistful of Quill's short, messy blond hair and rocked into his mouth instead.

With a groan around my cock, he moved both hands to clench the waistband of my pants and surrendered control like he always did, letting me drive myself crazy fucking his mouth.

My shadow heated and rolled under my skin, rising closer to the surface, feeding off of Quill's building pleasure. This wasn't as good as possessing Sawyer, but it was the next best thing as far as my shadow seemed to be concerned.

The thought tightened my chest, making my heart ache. Sawyer was off limits. Even if I hadn't sent him spiraling, questioning his identity, he was too young and Quill was the one I loved.

"Enough," I rasped, and I jerked his head off my cock.

He stared at me stunned, not knowing I'd really meant enough to my shadow and not him.

"You're wearing too much clothing." I pushed him up and his stunned expression darkened again with a desire that I knew was more than just my shadow's allure.

We'd been lovers with a more than casual relationship before I'd been infected, and I was grateful every day that he'd stuck by me, helping me through those hungry, desperate days, when my shadow and I hadn't yet come to terms with each other.

He shrugged out of his jerkin then tugged his shirt off slowly, revealing inch by inch his gorgeous lean-muscled abs and chest.

I licked my lips, my mouth going dry in anticipation even as my shadow jerked me upright. It had no patience for drawn out love making right now. It needed to ride Quill's release. Now.

I yanked off my own shirt, shoved Quill on his back, grabbed his pants, and — with a helpful rise of his hips — yanked them down to his boots.

He reached to start unlacing them but I pressed a hand against his chest pinning him down and licked a hot, wet path from the base of his cock to his tip, drawing a delicious gasp of pleasure.

Goddess, I wished my shadow wasn't so desperate and I could draw this out. I wanted Quill panting and begging, his eyes glazed with pleasure. I wanted to sear my love for him on his body and show him how much *I* needed him. Not just my shadow, but me.

I ran my fingers over his tip, covering them in precum before leaning forward. Slowly, I took him into my mouth while teasing the tight ring of muscle of his hole with my slicked finger.

He groaned and bucked, bumping his cock against the back of my throat, his breath ragged. His desire blazed into my shadow, inflaming my skin, and I sucked and licked, his cock hard and hot and heavy in my mouth while working one finger then two inside him.

"Fuck, Talon," he gasped, his fingers digging into my scalp. "Oh, fuck."

I pulled back, making him whimper at the loss of

my touch then pressed the head of my cock at his entrance. His mouth opened on a soft, deep, throaty groan that went straight to my balls, and his gaze was heavy with need.

Fuck, seeing him on the edge, about to come undone, was something I craved, again and again. I loved that look, those sounds, the feel of his body, tight and hot around me as I pushed inside him.

Then his eyes rolled back, his lids fluttering shut and my shadow billowed out of my skin and caressed him, teasing him more, building and devouring his pleasure.

Trembling, I buried myself deep inside him and leaned in to capture his mouth. He opened, letting me plunge my tongue inside, filling him in everyway I could.

His hard cock was trapped between us, and I rubbed myself against him as my hips started to pump, trying to draw out the most pleasure possible.

“Oh fuck, Talon. Yes,” he moaned into my mouth, as he grabbed fistfuls of my hair.

What little control I had vanished. My shadow took over and I pounded into him until he cried his release, his cum shooting over our chests, his muscles clenching around me, drawing out my own explosive orgasm.

My shadow curled in and around him then poured hot and satisfied back inside me and I collapsed on top of him, my muscles shaky and spent.

Gasping, he shifted so we could lie in each other's arms without suffocating, and he buried his face in my neck, breathing me in.

When I managed to get my breath back, I moved to sit up and give Quill some space, but his grip around me tightened.

"Stay with me like this while we talk with Ash," he said, his words making my heart flutter and my throat tighten.

He didn't mean it the way I wanted him to mean it.

"Of course."

I settled back down and a contented sigh slipped from his lips. Then he relaxed even more as he sent his spirit to the Garden.

"I'll stay with you like this forever," I told his unconscious body, knowing he couldn't hear me. "I love you."

I loved him so much it hurt. But he wanted a female mate so I'd never tell him the truth: that he was the one my soul cried for.

Even if I didn't have the shadow trapped inside me and it was safe for me to take a female mate, I wouldn't. I wanted Quill. My heart and soul and spark wanted Quill. He felt like home... just like Sawyer had.

CHAPTER 21
Sage

I WOKE in the Garden again with the aching, twisting need from Talon's magic only partially diminished despite touching myself and making myself come multiple times back in my bedroom in the Black Tower.

Great Father! I wanted to scream in frustration. Even with my body weak and trembling and filled with ice from his shadow, I still craved another release.

I'd barely managed to get myself under control when Lord Quill had returned to my room with a tray overflowing with food. And in the short time he'd been with me, my desire had been almost back to where I'd started when Lord Rider had pushed me into Lord Quill's arms and he'd carried me from the practice yard to my room.

It had taken everything I'd had to not stare at him

and not to react to the sensation zinging through me when he touched me. Even the panic induced by his interest about me — or rather Sawyer's sister — hadn't done much to ease my yearning for him.

Thankfully, no one sat on the bench on the other side of the pool where I'd woken in the Garden, and I didn't have to fend off Wells's and Crane's unwanted advances, or fight my attraction to Lord Rider or anyone else.

And as much as my body yearned to find Fantasy Man and have him satisfy me again, I couldn't forget what I'd decided last night, which was to stay focused on keeping Sawyer safe.

Giving in to my desire would only jeopardize my plans. The men here were looking for their mate and while I looked like I was fae in my spirit form, I wasn't fae and that could only spell trouble for me in my real body back in the Black Tower.

I couldn't risk them thinking I was their chance to be mated, and I certainly couldn't risk triggering whatever magic bound fae's souls together to create these bonded mate groupings.

And since I hadn't had a chance to figure out how to send my spirit back to my body, let alone not manifest my spirit into the Garden in the first place, I was going to have to avoid everyone until I returned to the Black Tower.

And that included Fantasy Man.

The evening breeze warmed my still ever-so-slightly too-cool skin and ruffled through my long hair. It carried the sound of men's voices and the sweet scent of flowers, drawing my attention to the gauzy green curtains separating the garden part of the Garden from the courtyard.

An unsettling mix of desire and fear twisted in my gut. I should leave, go deeper into the garden, and get as far away from the men gathered in the courtyard as possible, and yet that wouldn't help me if I ran into anyone.

I still knew nothing about fae and fae culture. I had no idea how long it was going to take me to figure out what was going on with me that made me wake every night in the Garden or how long it was going to take me to stop it from happening. I could try to hide every time I came here, but I always woke in the same spot close to the courtyard, and I was bound to be greeted again by Wells and Crane or other men like I had last night.

Lord Rider had mentioned something about putting the men in their place, but I didn't know what that meant and I couldn't just ask someone. I mean, I supposed I could, I just didn't know how strange the question would be.

Here in the Garden where I was a woman, I was sure it would be extremely strange. I was supposed to be familiar with fae culture.

And if I asked Kit or Payne back in the Black Tower where I was a man... probably strange as well.

Why would a man want to know how a woman was supposed to behave in someone else's culture?

Which meant I was going to have to figure it out by myself, and since I was here, the best way to do that was to observe how men and women interacted with each other.

There was a chance there wouldn't be any women in the courtyard since I couldn't remember seeing any of them last time, but then I'd been instantly swarmed by a group of men all bigger than me. Even if there weren't any women around, just watching the men was the best use of these unwanted visits. At the very least, maybe I'd get a better idea of who was safe to run into and who wasn't.

The catch would be to find a place where I could watch without drawing attention to myself. As soon as I stepped past those gauzy curtains, I'd be swarmed again.

I scanned the rolling lawn, the flowerbeds, and the stone path between me and the courtyard. The curtains undulated with the breeze, tangling around the statues of the fae women standing at the edge of the courtyard and revealing glimpses of the men inside.

There wasn't a good place to observe those inside while being unnoticed. At least not any place that didn't make it look like I was spying on them if I got caught.

And while yes, I *was* spying on them, I didn't want to look like I was sneaking around.

A stronger breeze rippled through the curtains, making the fabric canopy above the courtyard flutter, drawing my attention to the strange building beyond it.

It was hard to tell in the moonlight, but it looked like a castle and a tree had been mashed together in an impossible melding of stone and foliage like the stone-vine archway at the entrance of the grove.

I strolled across the lawn attempting to look casual while not following the path leading to the courtyard to try to get a better look at the building.

There were lights flickering among the leaves as well as against the fae's magical, almost perfectly clear glass windows at least five stories up, and I got a sense of wood and rope bridges hanging between the enormous branches.

Three men strode out of the courtyard and I shrunk back into the shadow of a tall shrub.

Unlike the previous night where every man had snapped his gaze to me the moment he'd left the courtyard, these three didn't even glance my way, and I could only hope that was because I wasn't out in the open and not because they were already mated and no longer had a strange attunement to know exactly where an unmated woman was.

If all unmated men did know exactly where I was, that would ruin my plan of trying to secretly observe them.

I hurried farther away from the entrance, circling the courtyard in the shadows until I reached where its canopy and curtains connected with the building, which was indeed half stone and half tree.

Here there was another path that led out of the courtyard and into the garden as well as a stone staircase with a hip-high railing that curled up around a wide tree trunk.

This close, I could now see that there were balconies one and two floors above the courtyard and above that, windows overlooking the courtyard as well.

The first level of balconies sat beneath the gauzy canopy, promising a perfect view of those inside, and while there was light and a handful of people in a couple of the balconies, the three smaller ones closest to the edge where I stood were dark and hopefully empty.

I hurried up the stairs into a strange half-tree half-stone hallway. More of the vines with the softly glowing white and pink flowers illuminated the space making it difficult to tell where tree ended and stone began. Beside me stood the dark, open archway to the first balcony while up ahead, two more archways down, light and laughter from the occupied balconies spilled into the passage.

I peeked into the first balcony just to make sure it really was empty then hurried inside. The space was deeper than I'd first thought with room for a delicately carved table and four chairs on one side near the back and a seating area with two couches on the other side near the railing at the front.

The dim light of two barely lit fae lanterns glimmered, one above the table and the other over the seating area, but I ignored them, leaving them at their lowest setting, and stepped up to the silver railing wrapped with vines and branches.

Just below the level of my balcony hung the lanterns for the courtyard with large metal shades reflecting the light down, keeping the balcony wrapped in shadows while offering me a perfect view of those below.

As expected, the courtyard was filled with fae men, all of them tall and beautiful and bigger than most humans. They were also stronger than human men, but now I knew the truth that only half of them had magic and, unlike the minstrels' tales, most of that magic wasn't overly powerful. That said, there was no way of telling just by looking at them who had powerful magic and who didn't.

The men sat in conversation areas or at tables or stood near the food and drink tables, all of them talking and laughing with each other. A couple in a darker corner away from the other conversation area were quietly making out, and no one seemed to notice or care.

With the exception that there was only one woman who was surrounded by three men and being ignored by everyone else — and the couple making out — the gathering below looked like the one social event I'd attended as a child when my mother had taken me and Sawyer to the royal court in Erellod to finalize her marriage to Edred.

A flicker of impossible golden sunshine caught my attention, and my gaze jumped across the room to Lord Quill and Talon sitting at a table in another out-of-the-way corner.

Seeing them made my pulse skip and the remaining desire from Talon's magic — that I'd so far managed to ignore — flared back to life.

They were eating and drinking and sharing a quiet conversation, their voices too soft for me to hear over the din of conversation from the other men, and I yearned for the feel of Talon's mouth on mine even if that meant his shadow's ferocious frozen power would steal all strength and heat from my body again.

Lord Quill nodded at something Talon said, sending a lock of golden hair spilling across his forehead.

Unlike Talon, his hair was short like Sawyer's — like mine now was. I'd thought that was unusual for a fae, but only about half of the fae in the Black Guard had long hair. And while those in the Garden were more likely to have the waist-length long hair that the minstrels' tales sung about, Lord Quill wasn't the only one in the courtyard with shorter hair.

I leaned against the railing, my body trying to draw closer whether I wanted to or not, and while I could chalk up my desire for Talon as a result of his shadow's magical allure, I couldn't explain my attraction to Lord Quill.

And I certainly couldn't explain the shock of something that always zinged through me whenever we touched.

There was something about him... about both of them that called to me, and the longer I sat there, the harder it was to remember that I needed to keep my distance from them.

I heaved my attention to the other side of the courtyard, determined to stop staring. I needed to practice not looking at them now or I was going to be a disaster tomorrow during training.

Great Father, how was I going to get through anything when even just thinking about Talon made the memory of his shadow's magic swell inside me?

I groaned with desire, but the heated need froze suddenly as a hint of unease flickered through me.

Someone was watching me.

CHAPTER 22
Sage

THE SENSE that someone watched me jolted through my body, and I glanced over my shoulder to see a man standing just inside the archway in such a way that he was barely visible, wreathed in shadows.

"You've got to stop making sounds like that," Fantasy Man said, his seductive tenor sliding against my senses and reigniting the remnants of Talon's magic.

"Is that really what you want?" I asked boldly, my voice husky.

Maybe I could have one more night with Fantasy Man, and *then* I could focus on ignoring my desire and sticking with my plan.

Shadows, what a terrible idea.

But the instant I thought it, my body heated, melting away the last of Talon's cold that had been chilling my insides. Light and heat flared from the spots around my neck and another soft groan escaped my lips before I could stop it.

"It's certainly not what you want," Fantasy Man said with a wry chuckle. "You should be down there finding some men who catch your fancy."

"Maybe I've already found someone," I replied.

He chuckled again, the sound teasing down my spine. "Ah, but just one isn't fun."

"Are you proposing we pick someone below to join us?" I asked, the words slipping out before I could stop them.

My cheeks heated with embarrassment and desire at the idea of being pleasured by multiple men at once like Lark, and I was grateful I hadn't bothered to make the fae lanterns brighter.

He hummed low in his throat, a non-answer to my question. "Take a look. There are a lot of interesting options tonight."

"Like who?" I leaned forward again and focused my attention on the courtyard below, hoping he'd step up behind me like he had the first night he'd caught me watching Lark and her mates.

"What are you attracted to?" he asked, his voice a sensual purr, suddenly close.

My breath caught in surprise. I hadn't even heard him move which meant he'd wanted me to notice him in the doorway.

A man who could move that silently could have stood in the hall's shadows and watched me all night without me knowing.

His chest brushed my back and he slid his hands up my bare arms, making me tremble with a need I wasn't going to be able to resist no matter what I wanted

"Falcon and Moor are quite handsome," he murmured in my ear.

"Yes, but what are they like?" I asked, my voice breathy.

Wells and Crane were handsome, too, but just being near them made me feel uncomfortable... unlike Fantasy Man.

Which didn't make any sense.

But then me being in the Garden and looking like a fae didn't make sense either.

Fantasy Man hummed again and teased his palms back down my arms, placing his hands over top of mine on the railing, pinning me in place. Not that I wanted to move.

"They'd make good mates," he replied.

Which meant I needed to stay far away from them.

Except everyone here, including Fantasy Man, thought I was looking for my mates, thought the marks around my neck were compelling me, so I couldn't just refuse Falcon and Moor without a good excuse.

And while I might be able to be hesitant about

Fantasy Man's suggestion, I knew enough now about the marks that if I really was fae, I couldn't outright deny them like I wanted to.

Not to mention by talking about Falcon and Moor and the other men in the courtyard, I might get a better understanding of how to behave. Maybe I could get a little information *and* a little satisfaction from Fantasy Man.

Oh, yes please!

"Good mates, hunh?" I asked. "What makes them good mate material?"

"Well, Falcon is handsome. Always a plus to wake up everyday to someone who's nice to look at." He pointed to a tall, thin fae with shoulder-length sandy-blond hair pulled back at the nape of his neck.

The man, Falcon, was almost as striking as Talon with an easy smile like Payne's, but I didn't feel compelled to stare at him like I did with Talon or Lord Quill or even Lord Rider.

"He's fun and good-natured and would make a good balance to whoever ends up as your first mate," Fantasy Man added.

Which implied that there was something special about first mates. Crane had mentioned something about letting Rider be my first mate as well, and from the stories I'd heard, it sounded like Blaze was Lark's first mate.

Were first mates supposed to be more aggressive

than other mates? Perhaps aggressive wasn't the word. More protective?

"He controls plant life," Fantasy Man said, sliding an arm around my waist and tugging me tighter against his body, his warmth adding to the heat inside me. "His magic isn't overly powerful, but every garden and farm could use a little magic so he's always in demand."

"Guess that means he'll be too busy for me," I said with an exaggerated sigh.

"I'm pretty sure he'd make time," Fantasy Man laughed then lowered his voice back to a sensual purr that made me clench my thighs together, aching with anticipation. "A man would have to be an idiot not to make time for you."

With my eyes closed, I tipped my head back, brushing my temple against his chin and melting into his embrace. "Again with that assumption that I'm a worthwhile person."

"I'm a pretty good judge of character."

He pressed his lips against my forehead and I resisted the urge to open my eyes. I didn't want to scare him away by trying to look at him.

My chest tightened with the hurt that he didn't want me to know him, but maybe he sensed that I wasn't what everyone here thought I was. And if I wanted one more night with him before I refocused on my plan to avoid everyone, then I needed to not try to push past his unspoken boundaries.

"So you've figured me out along with everyone else here and can say with certainty that Falcon would be a good match."

"Yep," he said with a chuckle. "Moor would be a good match, too. He's the big guy talking with Falcon."

"Oh? What makes Moor so special?"

"He has a huge cock," Fantasy Man said, punctuating his words by rolling his hips forward and pressing his hard length against my rear.

"And every woman needs a mate with a huge cock," I said, with a gasping laugh, my desire fluttering hot and needy and growing with every pound of my heart.

"He doesn't have the quickest wit but he makes up for it in bed." Fantasy Man's hand inched from my waist to my hip and he brushed his lips against my neck.

"You have firsthand experience with him?" I teased, imagining the biggest cock I could which turned into Talon's cock and the memory of his stunning, naked body.

"He's not my type, but I have a friend who used to swear by him."

"A friend, hunh?" I asked, my tone playfully skeptical even as my breath picked up.

What would Talon's cock feel like sliding into me? What would it feel like to really kiss him and not just have his mouth pressed against mine while his shadow fed?

"So this is second-hand information," I forced out, trying to drag myself back to the conversation. "You don't really know if Moor has a big cock. Your friend could have lied to you."

"Not about... *cocks*," he chuckled, emphasizing the word.

I shuddered, my thoughts now lurching to the cock I *had* experienced and how incredible it had felt to have Fantasy Man moving inside me.

Oh, shadows!

"Speaking of cocks..." I murmured, reaching up to tease my hand through his hair, needing more than just our banter and his embrace.

But he grabbed my fingers and set them back on the railing. "No touching. This is about you."

"What if I want to touch you?"

Except he hadn't let me touch him before, not when we'd first met and not while we'd been cuddling in the nook, which went hand in hand with him not wanting me to see or know him.

He grew still behind me.

Crap. That was a boundary I shouldn't have pushed. I knew that, but I'd forgotten myself, lost on the desire of feeling him inside me again.

"Sorry," I murmured. "I know that's not what we have."

"What do you think we have?" he asked, his voice as small and quiet as mine.

I tightened my grip on the railing. "Nothing, really."

And yet everything. He was the first man to show me what sex was supposed to feel like. The first man, other than my brother, who I'd really felt safe with.

"You don't want me as a mate," I said, which was kind of a relief since I didn't want to be mated either. And yet the realization made something deep inside me ache, something I couldn't put my finger on and not something I should be thinking about right now. "You just want a little fun."

I should have been shocked and horrified that Fantasy Man was using me just for sex. But he'd brought me so much pleasure, and some of it without any pleasure for himself, that the idea of just being with him for the sake of sex didn't bother me at all.

Lewin had been horrified to realize that fae men didn't have many opportunities to sleep with a fae woman, so it made sense that even if Fantasy Man didn't want a mate, he'd still be interested in sex.

And really, I was pretending to be my brother in the Black Tower and would eventually be found out. I didn't have high hopes that everything— hell that *anything* would work out for me.

Being with Fantasy Man might be the only time a man ever touched me with kindness.

Of course, if he didn't want me as a mate, did that mean we could keep having *fun*? There wouldn't be anything more between us so I didn't have to worry about forgetting my purpose.

Except would not wanting to be mated be enough to prevent a bond from forming between us?

CHAPTER 23
Sage

"It's not you," he said, his voice low, edged with that broken resignation that I'd heard when we'd been cuddling in the nook after having sex. "I'm not good mate material."

"I've felt your cock," I teased, trying to lighten the mood. "If the only thing that makes Moor a good mate is his size, then you have nothing to worry about."

"Moor's job isn't dangerous." He wrapped his arms around me and held me tight as if he didn't want to let me go. "And he hasn't had to kill anyone. You deserve someone who's soul isn't stained."

Except if that was what stained a soul, mine was just as stained.

The memory of Pylos's death flashed through me. My stepfather's armsmaster had tumbled over that mountain's edge with wild, desperate screams and had fallen to his death, and I hadn't given it a second thought. Sawyer and I had kept running until we were as safe as we could get under the circumstances, and then I'd gone to the Black Tower and become a Guardsman.

I hadn't had time to think about what I'd done or what I would have done if he hadn't fallen off that cliff, but I knew in my heart if the mountain hadn't killed him, I would have. I would have fought with everything I had and used every dirty trick I could think of because it had been his life or Sawyer's.

"If that's the requirement then Moor doesn't deserve me," I whispered. "I've killed someone, too." And I'd do it again if I had to.

"Accidents don't count, Red." He pressed his lips against the top of my head.

I didn't correct him. If I was really fae, Sawyer and I wouldn't have had to run for our lives. We wouldn't have watched our family die and been left with a stepfather who only saw us for what we could get him.

"I'm sorry you had to experience that, though," he murmured, his thumb tracing soft circles against my ribs as if he was trying to soothe me and didn't even realize it.

"And there you go being thoughtful again, just like making sure I came before you did even if that meant I disappeared before you were done," I murmured back.

"I'm not sure you've convinced me that you're bad mate material."

"Murder doesn't disqualify me?" he asked, his tone turning wry.

"You mentioned it in the same breath as you mentioned your dangerous job, so I doubt you just go around killing people for fun," I replied. "My father had been forced to kill a lot of men, evil men who hurt people. It's all about your intent."

And everything inside me said Fantasy Man didn't have evil intent. Which was crazy. My imagination could just be turning him into someone I wanted him to be, not who he really was.

But that thing in my soul assured me that I was right. I could trust him. I was safe with him.

"Your father?" he asked, making my thoughts stutter.

Oh, crap. I was supposed to have multiple fathers and an enormous extended family. Except I didn't want to make up a bunch of lies. Sure, I was going to avoid Fantasy Man and every other man in the Garden after this, but I still couldn't risk telling lies then forgetting them and getting caught.

"He… upheld the law." Which was true and hopefully vague enough that he wouldn't push for more information. "So, what else is so horrible about you? You hog the covers in bed?"

"Yep. I roll myself into a cocoon and snore like

thunder all night long," he said with a chuckle, thankfully not fighting me on the change in conversation.

"So extra blankets and cotton for my ears. Not a problem."

"All right. Fine. If I drink too much, I sing bawdy songs all night long," he warned.

"What a coincidence! So do I," I shot back in mock surprise. "And I have a horrible singing voice."

"I doubt you have a bad voice." He dipped in and brushed his lips against my temple. "Not if the sounds you make when I touch you are anything to go by," he purred, his tone low and sensual, making it clear that by touch he really meant sex.

"I'm not sure I believe you," I replied, my voice husky with need. "I think you should *touch* me again to prove it."

"I think we should find someone down there to touch you so I can have an objective opinion," he murmured. "If Falcon and Moor don't catch your interest what about—"

The curtain on the far side of the courtyard swept open, and Wells and Crane strode inside exuding confidence and that hungry danger that made my skin crawl.

A shiver ran down my spine at the memory of them trapping me between them, chilling some of the desire Fantasy Man had reignited. I shrank back, pressing myself even closer to him, afraid they'd look up and see me.

"Not Wells or Crane, hunh?" Fantasy Man said, his voice darkening.

I opened my mouth to say I wouldn't want either of them as a husband let alone touching me but managed to stop myself. I still didn't know how forthright I could be, and for all I knew Fantasy Man was friends with them.

"I probably didn't get the best first impression of them," I hedged. "I was disoriented my first time here."

"Or maybe your first impression was the right one. What do your instincts say?"

That I could trust Fantasy Man even though I knew nothing about him and that— "Wells and Crane are dangerous. And not like how Blaze or Rider are dangerous. It's something— I can't explain it. There's just something..."

"Wrong about them?" he finished for me.

"Yes."

The two men headed to the table with the pitchers of beverages and empty glasses, exchanging friendly greetings with everyone as if I was the only one who thought there was something wrong with them.

A smaller man — at least smaller compared to the other fae but still bigger than the average human man — joined them. Crane poured him a drink as the man said something and Wells threw his head back and laughed a deep, free laugh that made my skin crawl.

"It must just be me because no one else is acting like there's anything wrong with them." Except that wasn't true. Talon had tensed and Lord Quill looked worried.

It was a subtle change in posture and expression, and I shouldn't have been able to see it since I didn't know either man very well, but I just *knew* they sensed there was something wrong with Wells and Crane as well.

"They're very good at hiding their true nature, but you're not the only one who's noticed." He tightened his grip on me, his body curling forward slightly as if he was trying to protect me. "They won't hurt you, but it's probably best to avoid being alone with them."

"I've already figured that out."

And I had serious doubts about whether they'd hurt me or not. Fae culture might think I was precious because I was a woman, but Wells and Crane acted more like the human men I was familiar with, and those men hadn't hesitated to hurt me.

The curtain swept aside again and this time a woman entered. A man who was almost as gorgeous as Talon followed her, but she was the one who drew every eye in the courtyard.

And rightly so. She was stunning, dressed in a flowing white and gold gown that accentuated her full breasts and curvy hips and had a plunging neckline just like mine that revealed her mating marks. Most of them were pale yellow, a match to her blond hair, but a few of them were dark red, which I knew had to indicate something, I just wasn't sure what.

Most of the men headed toward her as if mesmerized by her presence. Wells's hungry smile grew, but he didn't join the crowd with the others, which, given how aggressively he and Crane had pursued me, surprised me.

The woman smiled and laughed and radiated a glowing confidence not at all intimidated by the press of the much larger men all around her. She looked men in the eyes, teased and flirted with some while flatly refusing or even ignoring others not worried about the repercussions of saying no or being rude.

It was astounding. I'd never seen a woman act like that before. I had no idea how she stayed so calm and confident in the face of all that masculine hunger, let alone glowed with pleasure from it.

Was that how I was supposed to behave? It went against everything I'd been taught. If I flatly told Wells and Crane no, would they stop pursuing me?

She said something to one of the men who broke apart from the group with a huge smile and headed to the drinks table and poured her a drink while she pushed farther into the courtyard.

The men all moved with her, parting to make way,

as if her very presence commanded them. Just a look or a smile or a refusal and the men obeyed. Some looked disappointed but no one raised a hand to her or was sharp with her or told her she wasn't behaving properly.

"She's incredible," I said, as mesmerized by her grace and confidence as the men around her were.

"Ember does make an entrance," Fantasy Man said, his tone wry.

"But you're not interested?" I asked, a little surprise and yet strangely satisfied that he wasn't. "She's gorgeous."

"I'm bad mate material," he reminded me with a shrug then he brushed his lips against the back of my neck, just a whisper of a touch but it stole my breath and made my heart race. "And you're gorgeous, too."

"Not like that, I'm not," I said, my voice husky as I melted into him. She was a goddess among her worshipers. "She's not afraid of any of them."

"And you are?" he asked, except I had a feeling he'd already figured out that being swarmed like that wouldn't light me up like it did Ember but would make me want to run away.

"They're all just so..." Hungry, desperate, overwhelming. "Intense."

And while Fantasy Man also seemed hungry, his hunger inflamed my desire.

Heat swelled in my marks and curled in my chest,

and I ached with need inspired by Talon's magic but also my own need for Fantasy Man, for how he made me feel the other night.

"The Garden can be a little much at the beginning," he said his tone low and sensual. He skimmed a hand up my ribs and teased the edge of my breast, stealing my breath for a heart-pounding moment. "But Ember has been searching for her mates for a while now. She bonded her first mate a few years ago but hasn't had much luck finding the others, so she's had lots of practice coming to the Garden and being greeted like this."

I shuddered at the thought of spending years showing up at the Garden and being surrounded by all those hungry men. "It'll take more than a few years for me to feel comfortable being mobbed like that."

"I doubt it'll take you years to find your mates." His fingers brushed closer to my breasts, and I tensed in anticipation. "A catch like you, willing to put up with a cover-hog who snores and sings rude songs when he's drunk will be fully mated before you even know it."

Better yet, I'd find a way to stop waking up in the Garden and avoid being mated at all...

But after tonight.

After I'd had one final night with my Fantasy Man.

CHAPTER 24
Sage

THE MAN GETTING Ember a drink pushed through the crowd, parting it to return to her side, giving Ember a perfect view of Talon and Lord Quill sitting at their table in the corner. Her smile grew even brighter, and she confidently strode up to Talon, not even giving Lord Quill a second glance.

A hint of something that I wasn't going to call jealousy twisted around my heart.

Really, it was really anger that she was outright ignoring quiet, charming Lord Quill and not because she looked like she wanted to devour Talon. Neither man was mine and weren't ever going to be mine no matter how much I couldn't stop staring at them. That, and Talon's magic was probably drawing her to him. She couldn't help herself, just like I couldn't.

Except her expression wasn't of someone caught up

in the magic of Talon's allure, it was of someone determined to have her way with him.

And as if thinking about it gave it strength, the remnants of Talon's magic inside me surged, drawing a soft moan from my lips and making Fantasy man hum in pleasure.

"This should be entertaining," he whispered. His hot breath feathered across my cheek and spiraled around my Talon-inspired desire, sinking straight to my aching core. "Ember has been trying to get Talon since her marks appeared."

"But not his friend?" I moaned.

Shadows! Fantasy Man and I were still having our playful banter, but our desires had taken control of our bodies.

"He's not as striking... as Talon," I said, my thoughts starting to muddle, "but he's still handsome and he... looks kind."

"He is."

Fantasy Man's fingers rose higher to the neckline of my dress and skimmed over my exposed marks. Light and heat flared from them, and searing, liquid heat pooled low within me.

"Quill is a good man. Perfect mate material except for the fact that he doesn't have any magic." A hint of sadness crept into Fantasy Man's tone. "Even if Ember wasn't interested in having the prettiest men in the Garden, she wouldn't ever consider him."

Which was absolutely cruel, and it made my heart hurt to think that most women probably ignored him because of his lack of magic.

Had he even been with a fae woman, or did they all treat him like Ember did? Was that why he was so interested in me — as Sawyer's sister — because he was never going to have a relationship with a fae woman and he'd resigned himself to having one with a human?

Of course, if no magic meant he'd never be mated, he was someone I might be able to turn to for sex if I couldn't purge the rest of Talon's magic from my body.

Ember said something and trailed her fingers up Talon's arm. A spike of jealousy — shadows be damned it *was* jealousy — made me grind my teeth, despite my rising desire for Fantasy Man.

Great Father, I was losing my mind. Talon wasn't mine. I'd just gotten an enormous dose of his shadow's magic. That was all. Besides, his body language was clear and I had no reason to be jealous. Talon wasn't interested in her despite Ember doing her best to get him in bed with her.

I clutched the railing and Fantasy Man slipped his fingers inside my dress and palmed my breast.

My need snapped and everything within me focused on him. I reveled in the feel of his body pressed behind me, his erection hard against my rear, his hand hot and demanding on my breast. It could have only gotten better if Talon, with his intoxicating magic, joined us.

Through my partially closed lids, I saw Talon shake his head. Ember leaned closer, her palms on the table giving him a perfect view down the front of her dress, and light flickered from her yellow mating marks.

But instead of looking interested, he looked upset and said something that made her jerk upright, looking like he'd slapped her, reminding me of how sharp he'd been when he'd found Rider talking to me.

"I think that might be a record," Fantasy Man said with a chuckle, the sound vibrating through me, filling me with light and heat. "Talon's sharp, but he's usually not that sharp that quickly."

"I'd beg to differ," I moaned, letting my eyes fully close on the courtyard and focusing solely on the sensations Fantasy Man was building inside me. "His only words to me were sharp and he said them right away. But it's nice to know I'm not the only woman he's rude to."

"Oh, he's rude to every woman. He doesn't want a mate but he's too pretty for his own good." Fantasy Man plucked my nipple.

With a gasp, I leaned into him, rolling my head back onto his shoulder and giving him my body.

"So, you tried to get him in your bed?"

I wish I had—

No.

No, I didn't.

Because the only version of me he was possibly interested in was Sawyer and after his shadow attacked me, I had a feeling whatever we had was going to be over. The version of me in the Garden hadn't even had a chance at a friendship let alone anything more.

Except Lord Rider and Talon had said no one else knew about his shadow, and while I suspected he'd be able to hide it for a little while from a lover, I doubted he'd be able to hide it forever. Which was why he was rude to women.

He didn't want a mate because he couldn't risk her or her other mates not understanding the nature of his shadow. And unlike Quill, his magic made him a possible mate. Did that mean he couldn't even indulge in a casual relationship?

"I was actually with Lo—" I bit my lip, stopping myself before I put *lord* in front of Rider because he wasn't a lord in the Garden. "I was with Rider. It was my first night here and I honestly thought it was all a dream. He was kind and... well, Talon wasn't."

"Rider was kind?" Fantasy Man asked, his voice thick with his own desire as his hand on my thigh slowly inched my dress up. "I'll have to mark that in my calendar. How many words did he manage to say to you?"

"I think you're being too hard on him." Sure he was a gruff, tough commander, but he was also extremely protective. He hadn't needed to help me my first two nights in the Garden nor send me to my room after Talon's shadow attacked me. "I think everyone is. His sister and Talon both gave him a hard time just for talking with me."

"That's because he never talks to women." Fantasy Man reached the hem of my dress and slipped his hot hand up my bare thigh, heading straight to where I needed him. "He's as interested in a mate as Talon is. Or at least he was..."

Given how quickly Rider had vanished when I'd asked him to show me the Garden— "I'm pretty sure that's still the case."

Fantasy Man teased his fingers into my curls while his hand on my breast worked my nipple into a tight aching bud.

I arched into his touch, clinging to the railing and fighting the urge to let go and touch him.

"Oh Fa—" I gasped, swallowing the rest of the word so I wouldn't invoke the human's deity.

"Are you sure he's not interested?" Fantasy Man teased, dipping his fingers into my soaked folds and groaning in pleasure.

The sound shuddered through me, and my breath hitched. The heat and pressure from the mating marks I shouldn't have had swelled and the remnants of Talon's magic only made it stronger.

"Shadows. Can we please stop talking about Rider

and Talon and all the men in the courtyard? I need you."

"I know, Red," he murmured against my neck. "The compulsion from your marks is powerful, but I've got you. I can ease some of the pressure until you're ready to go down there."

He pushed a finger inside me and rubbed the slickened pad of his thumb against the sensitive nub at my entrance.

I moaned and squirmed against his grip, not caring that someone could look up from the courtyard and see us. My need was too strong. It overwhelmed everything, my worry that I wasn't behaving like a fae woman, my fear of the sexually hungry men below, and my dread that my soul might bind one of them to me.

Fantasy Man worked me up quickly, thankfully not torturing me this time by bringing me to the edge of a release but not letting me crash over. I trembled in his embrace, my legs barely holding me up, my grip on the railing turning my knuckles white.

With a soft, sensual groan, he pushed the back of my dress up and ran his hands over my naked butt.

"Goddess, you're so beautiful," he said, his voice aching with a longing that made my heart break.

But before I could make my mind work enough to ask him about it, he tugged my hips back, nudged my legs open, and pressed the tip of his cock against my entrance.

My breath stalled completely and the light and heat for my marks blazed, lighting around my face for a moment.

Talon glanced up, thankfully the only one who seemed to notice, but his attention locked on me for a heart-pounding moment as if, even though the light from my marks around me had dimmed and the light in the courtyard was shining in his eyes, he could see me.

Then Fantasy Man pushed into me in a slow, sensual stroke and everything vanished with the incredible feeling of him filling me.

Oh, yes. Oh Great Father, yes. I trembled, overwhelmed by him, his presence, his heat, his cock, and pressed my forehead against my hands, fighting to stand against the onslaught of sensation.

He buried himself all the way and stopped, his breath as ragged as mine, washing over the back of my neck.

"Come here," he said. "I don't think either of us will be able to keep standing." He wrapped a strong arm around my waist and lowered us to the couch thankfully right behind him.

I ended up straddling him, my legs spread wide, and he grasped my hips. His large hands were big enough that he could easily steady me while I rose and fell in rhythm to his thrusts and tease the nub at my entrance.

I mewled and gasped, trying to keep my noises quiet, but I spiraled faster and faster toward an incredible release and it became impossible to concentrate on anything.

Talon's magic entwined with whatever magic was in the mating marks, and my need roared into an inferno around my heart and in my core as Fantasy Man's thrusts grew faster and harder.

My breath came in short, sharp gasps and my desire spiraled tighter and tighter and tighter, until I crashed over the edge, stars exploding behind my lids.

I bit my lip, fighting my cry of pleasure, and Fantasy Man thrust fiercely, chasing his own release. He tensed, and with a long, low, masculine groan that sent me soaring to new heights, he came hard inside me.

"Oh wow," I gasped, the world spinning around me even though my eyes were closed and I couldn't actually see it moving.

"I told you I'd take care of you, Red," he said, holding me tight against him.

"I knew you would." I relaxed against him, a warm comfortable heaviness sinking in me even as my throat tightened with sadness.

This had to be our last time. I couldn't risk accidentally binding him to me. But Great Father, I didn't want it to be.

Maybe if I never saw him or never learned his name we wouldn't be able to accidentally mate. If Talon's magic was going to continue affecting me along with the mating marks I had in my spirit form, then avoiding all men in the Garden was going to be hard.

I didn't know if I had it in me to resist the compulsion and I couldn't risk my will power breaking when I was with someone who's life I could ruin.

"It's all right," he murmured as if he sensed my worries. "Just let it go."

Except it wouldn't be all right. I craved him more now than I ever did before.

But the darkness of exhaustion called to me, and I slipped back into my body in the Black Tower, fully satiated, no longer cold from Talon's magic, but more confused than ever about what I should do about Fantasy Man and the Garden and everything.

CHAPTER 25
Ash

One day. One fucking day. That's all I lasted before I caught a glimpse of red hair heading up the stairs to the balconies overlooking the courtyard, and I was drawn like a fucking moth.

I screamed into my pillow in my bedroom at the Black Tower like I had the previous morning.

I'd been fine.

Fine, damn it!

The previous night I'd managed to have a meeting with Rider, Talon, and Quill and leave right away despite the ache in my chest urging me to look for her. But last night Talon had suggested we stay in the courtyard to wait for Rider on the off chance that he'd actually pull his shit together and make it to our nightly meeting.

I'd been an idiot and agreed even though I knew

that if Rider's rage had been enough for his wolf to take over, we wouldn't have seen him until morning.

And by the time I'd realized staying was the worst idea ever, my insides had twisted tight with my need to find Red and reconnect with her, and I could barely breathe, let alone think.

Then I'd caught that glimpse of her heading up the stairs and that was it. I was gone. My heart had pounded so hard I hadn't heard what either Talon or Quill had said. I'd just gotten up, left them, and followed her.

Goddess above! What the fuck was wrong with me?

I used to be in control of myself and my urges. I knew what my fate was and while I hadn't been fine with it, I'd accepted it. And then a stunning redhead stumbled into my life, her emerald eyes wide with awe and fear, and had turned everything upside down.

She'd even figured out that I didn't want her to see me or know my name and had accepted it, and I hadn't gotten a sense that she was just humoring me and hoping that her marks would bind my soul to hers. It was like she understood that I wasn't ready to be seen and probably wouldn't ever be ready.

Of course, from the way she looked at the men in the courtyard, she wasn't ready either. I'd known before she'd confessed to me that the men below made her nervous, which made me wonder who she really was.

I still didn't know her name — I wasn't even sure she'd told anyone in the Garden her name since all my methods of information gathering had failed to discover it — but that didn't really matter. She was Red to me and I was fine with that... because if I knew her name, it would be even harder to ignore my desire for her.

Which was damn hard to begin with, because everyone in the Garden was talking about her, talking about her sudden appearance and then how she wasn't coming to the courtyard to find her mates. And that wasn't like any fae woman they'd ever met.

Even one who wasn't ready for her mates knew the only way to relieve the pressure of her mating marks was to give in to her desire and hopefully find her mates quickly so she could move on with the rest of her life. And the best way to do that was to go to the courtyard.

But she was afraid of the attention — and I got the sense she was afraid of attention in general — but also afraid because that attention came from men.

Which was even more confusing. I'd never met a woman that afraid of men. They'd been surrounded by us all their lives, and while Red was a little smaller than the average female, she should have been used to it... unless, of course she was from one of the sects that sheltered their women from outsiders.

But if that was the case, once they learned her

spirit was manifesting in the Garden they'd have put a stop to it until she was fully mated and wanted to have children, since fae women could only conceive in the Garden.

Perhaps her family hadn't figured out that she was manifesting already. If men made her nervous, I doubted she'd tell anyone she was going to the Garden.

But she wouldn't be able to keep it a secret for much longer. Her marks were overflowing with power and her need to mate would soon make it impossible for her to concentrate on anything else and she'd be discovered.

Goddess, that couldn't come soon enough.

Except the moment I thought that, my heart clenched. My soul still thrummed with the power of the connection I'd made with her when I'd buried myself in her a second time. It was like life and light and magic and certainty exploding inside me, more powerful with her than with any woman I'd been with.

Of course, maybe that was just because it had been too long since I'd actually been with a fae woman, and I'd forgotten just how powerful and addicting the connection I made was.

I groaned, my cock hardening at the memory. I could still see the blaze of light from her marks dancing across the back of my lids and hear the moans of pleasure that had slipped from her lips. Her need had been so strong, the power billowing from her marks and rippling through her spirit form, I was a little surprised she hadn't thrown herself at me the moment I'd let her know I was watching her.

I'd tried to get her to consider some of the men below, but I'd ended up flirting with her instead, and then the power in her marks had increased as the magic from Talon's shadow caught her — even though he'd insisted that after attacking Sawyer it was fully fed.

With her fear of the men below, I'd known she would have stayed on the balcony and tried to take care of her desires by herself like she had when I'd found her in the nook, and I hadn't been able to just walk away.

That and my body had taken over even before my mind had realized what it was doing. I'd only added to her desire, and I wasn't going to leave her wanting. I might lie and cheat and steal and kill in cold blood to protect the realms, but I wasn't cruel. Not when I could help it.

Fuck. I hadn't wanted our time together to end. I'd wanted to make her come again and again until I'd released as much power from the marks as possible if only to give her time to find her courage. But her spirit form had rippled, heavy exhaustion — another curious anomaly that usually only happened to men in strenuous occupations — and she'd turned to smoke and vanished.

And now I was back in my bed in the Black Tower, once again aching for a connection I wasn't going to have, my cock and balls tight, screaming for another fucking release.

I rolled onto my back, pushed my blanket aside, and squeezed the base of my cock, trying to get myself back under control.

I had to pull my shit together, but I really didn't want to deal with Mikel and his plans to turn Sawyer into a man, especially now that Talon had incapacitated him into missing yesterday's training. They were going to go harder on the boy now that it was clear Rider was giving him special treatment.

Of course, from the look of the boy when I'd passed him on my way to the running trail, I doubt he'd been able to stand let alone run or fight and it had been a good call sending him back to his room.

Changing the day's lesson from daggers to wrestling, however, was a terrible call. I knew why Rider had done it. There'd been no point in testing Sawyer's wrestling abilities. The boy would have lost every fight until he'd been pitted against Tyon, and even then, if Tyon got in a lucky grab, the chef's assistant could use his extra weight and just sit on him. I doubted Sawyer had a high enough skill level to deal with someone twice his weight.

The pressure in my cock grew instead of subsiding

like I'd hoped by thinking about work, and the memory of Red's hot, wet sheathe flooded me.

I bit back a groan and slid my hand up to my tip where I was already leaking precum.

Despite her fear of the men in the courtyard, she'd leaned into my embrace and fully trusted me. She'd trusted me from the beginning, and I hadn't realized how special that was until we'd been flirting over the men in the courtyard last night.

And as soon as she saw me, she'd be afraid.

I had to keep reminding myself of that. I'd never been handsome like Talon, merely passable in my appearance, and now I wasn't even nice to look at. What woman wanted to wake up beside someone as scarred as me every morning?

Red, maybe, a tiny voice whispered inside me. *She's accepted everything else you've asked of her.*

But I couldn't let myself hope. I'd hoped before. I'd had a lover before I'd been burned, had thought she'd known me, known what kind of man I was on the inside. But being handsome on the inside hadn't mattered to her.

And now I wasn't handsome. Inside or out.

I pumped my hand up and down my length, unable to stop myself from imagining I was back inside Red.

I fantasized that she'd stayed and I'd made her come again, playing with that amazing sensitive nub until I was hard and ready to go again. Then I'd take her slowly for our second time. I'd lie her on the couch, capture her lips with mine, and breathe in her every moan. I'd savor the feel of our naked bodies brushing against each other, of her nipples, tight buds teasing my chest, and I'd fall into those emerald eyes, her face lit up from the power of her marks, as I made her moan with pleasure.

My cock swelled and I came into my hand and on my naked chest, but my release was nothing compared to what it had been with Red. It was empty and aching and only partially satisfying, and I had days to go before this rotation was done and I could get to the pleasure house in Lehyrst.

And even then, would another woman help me? She wouldn't be fae. My soul wouldn't connect with hers.

She wouldn't be Red.

Fuck.

Fuck fuck fuck.

CHAPTER 26

Ash

THE FIRST BELL RANG, telling me it was time to get up and get to work. If I hadn't been stuck pretending to be Ambrose the novice, I'd have headed straight to the practice yard and challenged every Guardsman there to a fight — and encouraged them to come at me two and three at a time. Rider wasn't the only one who vented his frustration and anger through physical activity, although his need was usually a lot stronger than mine. It had been a long time since I'd needed a good fight to clear my head... not since that long year after I'd been burned and I'd realized I'd lost any chance of having a mate.

The memory of Red's face illuminated by the red glow of her marks slammed into me.

She'd laid her head back on my shoulder, her eyes

closed and her lips parted in pleasure, her expression one of absolute bliss and trust.

I had to tell Rider I couldn't meet in the Garden anymore. It was the only way to save myself.

Except I had to go back to the Garden tonight to tell him that or risk revealing myself. And as much as a part of me thought telling Rider I was Ambrose was worth it to stop the torture of seeing Red, if he started treating me differently because he knew the truth, I could lose Mikel's trust and then I'd have no idea when or how he and his friends were going to turn Sawyer into a man.

Which meant I had to keep making my reports in the Garden whether I wanted to or not.

Goddess be damned. I hadn't hated my life this much since I'd been burned.

What I wouldn't give to go back to the Jerika family's attempts to murder each other to control the family's small but wealthy march. There were enough players in that mess to keep me fully distracted and on my toes watching out for assassins and poisoned food.

Footsteps hurrying in the hall outside my bedroom reminded me that I needed to get up, get something to eat, and get to my morning chores. Because I was supposed to be a soldier, I'd been assigned to the smithy for this rotation's duties along with Lander, the smith. He'd had three young children and a wife when his name had been drawn in the human's lottery that selected their Guardsmen and was another one of the novices that Rider, Talon, and Quill were concerned about.

I'd been thrilled to be assigned morning chores with him just to keep an eye on him, since — because no one knew who I really was — I usually wasn't assigned chores with the men I needed to keep an eye on. Lander was a skilled smith, so he'd been assigned helping Heath, the Black Tower's senior smith, but I'd been stuck with sitting outside the forge sharpening weapons and mending hilts and handles which wasn't physically aggressive enough for my current mood.

I got dressed, grabbed my breakfast, and sat with Mikel, Durand, and Hamelin. Bramwell joined us a few minutes later, his blond hair damp and dripping onto the shoulders of his jerkin.

He, like the others — and most of the men around me for that matter — had an orange on his tray, the Guard's attempt to silently remind Lord Sawyer of Herstind March of his place at the Black Tower. Someone had noticed the boy had had an orange with every meal and they'd decided that was one pleasure he wasn't going to get again. It was a small act, but on top of the not-so-accidental bumps and the snide comments, it was going to wear down whatever spark the boy had.

The thought of sparks made me think of Red and the spark she'd let me glimpse when we'd flirted.

Which wasn't something I should be thinking about.

"Did you see *the lord* in the baths?" Durand asked, his dark gaze sweeping over the men in line waiting to enter the kitchen.

"No." Bramwell dug his nail into his orange and pulled back a chunk of peel. "Do you think he's still lounging in his room on the Lord Commander's orders?"

"Wouldn't surprise me," Mikel huffed as the boy in question quietly stepped into the great hall and joined the line. "Well, look who looks absolutely fine."

My pulse leaped at the sight of his red hair even though it wasn't as vibrant as Red's, and I strained to focus on the boy and not think of *her.*

Goddess, please. I have to stop thinking of her.

The men in front of Sawyer glanced down at him, making the boy stiffen, but he met the Guardsman's gaze head on and squared his shoulders instead of dropping his gaze like he had on his first day here. The much larger human Guardsman rolled his eyes at him then turned to face forward again.

"He still hasn't learned his lesson," Hamelin said with a sigh. "A little respect would go a long way."

Except I doubted that. It didn't matter what Sawyer did, the men were going to make sure he knew they were pissed at him and there wasn't anything he could do about it. And while the others probably saw an arrogant, defiant young lord in that exchange, I saw a boy determined to make the best of a bad situation.

I also saw pain in his expression when he'd straightened.

It was subtle, hidden behind an emotionally flat mask that verged on arrogant, but it was there, and when the line moved forward and he moved two steps with it, it was obvious that he was in pain. The kind of pain that came from too much exertion and not enough rest.

Of course, like most novices, he probably wasn't used to the physical demands of being a Guardsman. That was why most novices were given the easier chores to help them build their endurance during their first few rotations.

But Sawyer had been assigned one of the more physically demanding chores and, added to the rigors of combat training, he was probably sore in places he'd never been sore before.

"Looks like he's recovered from whatever his *condition* was yesterday," Durand said, his tone clear that he hadn't believed there was anything wrong with him despite seeing the boy on the ground white as a sheet and looking like he was going to puke.

"I'm told Rider will bring the bags of rocks again,"

Mikel said around a mouthful of bread. "We need to make sure it's Sawyer running the extra lap."

The others nodded their agreement.

"Easiest way to do that is to make sure he doesn't cross the log over the stream," Durand said. "The banks are too tall and steep for him to climb up without help, so he'll have to go up or down stream to find his way out."

Sawyer and his red hair vanished into the kitchen and my gaze leaped to the other side, waiting for him to step back into sight.

"How are we making sure he doesn't cross?" Hamelin asked. "So far, he's made it across every time we've run the trail."

"One of us will have to bump him in," Mikel said.

They continued talking about how Sawyer's arrogance disgusted them and what they thought Rider was going to be testing and training us on that afternoon. I dragged my attention away from the boy and tried to listen to their conversation, but my mind kept jumping back to Red and her sounds and how she felt and how my soul now felt empty and cold.

The second bell rang and I headed to the forge to do a morning of odd jobs. Lander was even more withdrawn than yesterday, his eyes empty as he went through the movements of repairing broken and chipped blades under Heath's supervision. I hadn't seen him at the morning meal, but then I hadn't seen much of anything at the morning meal, although from his gaunt expression and gray complexion, I suspected he hadn't eaten. And he likely hadn't eaten the evening meal last night, either.

He stepped out of the forge and added a newly mended broadsword to my pile. His gaze slid blankly over the dozen men working in the baily then landed on Sawyer struggling with a wheelbarrow filled with soiled hay. The boy moved at half the speed he had his first official morning as a novice and struggled to keep the wheelbarrow from tipping over as he pushed it across the bailey.

"My nephew is twelve and he's as big as that boy," Lander said, his voice heavy with resignation. "I'd bet everything I have that he's not sixteen." He released a heavy sigh. "Or I suppose he spent most of his childhood sick. Pypa spent her first four years so sick we thought everyday that we were going to lose her. She's better, but she's smaller than the other girls her age."

Lander went back inside the forge without waiting for a response, but I would have bet everything I had that Lander's first assumption was right. Except if the boy wasn't going to come out and tell the truth, there wasn't anything Rider could do about it.

For the rest of the morning, I tried to focus on my real and fake-novice jobs, watching the novices and looking out for trouble among the ranks, but my mind kept returning to Red over and over again and by the time the third bell had rung announcing the midday meal, my cock was so hard it hurt.

Frustrated, I hurried back up to my room and jerked off again. But while that managed to deal with the pain in my cock, it didn't do anything for the root of the problem: the fact that I couldn't stop thinking about Red, about how she felt and sounded and—

Goddess damned fucking shadows!

CHAPTER 27
Ash

LUNCH WAS the same as breakfast. Sawyer's red hair made my heart leap and my thoughts jerk back to Red and it took everything I had just to stay focused on my fucking job.

The boy kept his head up while in line, the men around him gave him dark looks, and he grabbed some food from the kitchen then promptly left, not bothering to stay and eat in the great hall, while Mikel solidified his plan for getting Sawyer into the stream to ensure he finished the run last.

Of course, Mikel's plan hinged on Sawyer and everyone else not telling Rider what happened, but I was pretty sure Mikel had already figured out no one, including Sawyer, would say anything. The boy would take whatever the other men dished out without complaint just like he was taking everything else, and Mikel was smart enough to realize that.

Then the fourth bell rang, and my schedule finally gave me something that might burn away my aching need for Red.

I practically leaped from the table to put my dirty dishes in the bin at the back of the great hall, and Mikel flashed me a wicked grin, mistaking my eagerness to run for an eagerness to put Sawyer in his place.

"You ready?" Mikel asked us as we jogged out of the castle to the practice grounds, his voice pitched so that only the four of us could hear him.

Bramwell grunted and Durand gave a tight nod.

All in all, the plan was simple. It wasn't a tactical masterpiece, but it would work. Simple meant there were less things to go wrong. Bramwell was to run behind Sawyer, while Durand and I were to get in the boy's way just before the log bridge so Bramwell could bump him in. Mikel and Hamelin were to wait on the other side of the stream just in case Sawyer managed to get past us.

With luck, the boy would be in the water before he fully realized what had happened, and Mikel and his friends would feel satisfied that they were teaching him a lesson.

Without a doubt there would be other lessons, but if they all stayed at this level, no one's life would be in danger and the men would eventually be satisfied that Sawyer had paid for his mistake.

We reached the large stones marking the beginning of the running trail where the other novices, including Sawyer, waited. Once again, just catching a glimpse of his hair made my pulse leap and the memory of Red gasping with pleasure flooded me.

Fuck. I gritted my teeth. *Concentrate on the job. Stop thinking of her. Just Goddess damn stop thinking of her!*

Rider stood just to the side of the stones with the two bags of rocks at his feet. With a grunt, he crossed his arms and swept his gaze over us. His stance, not to mention his dark glare, made him look even more imposing and commanding, and while I was sure the others thought he was still pissed off from yesterday's disrespect by Mikel and Durand, I could tell that the night of hunting had actually eased some of the tension from his body. Not all, but at least he wasn't on the verge of shifting and ripping out someone's throat.

Then Talon and Quill came out the pasture gate, drawing Rider's attention and Sawyer's. The boy jerked his gaze to his feet then up to the stone as if he remembered he didn't want to look down, then shifted from one foot to the other clearly uncomfortable.

As Talon got closer, Sawyer grew tenser, his gaze locked on the mouth of the running trail, but I couldn't tell if his reaction was because Talon's allure was still affecting him or if he didn't know how to react to Talon in the face of what had happened.

And while it should have been the latter because his shadow had fed deeply from Sawyer, his allure had still affected Red last night despite them not making eye contact.

Of course, Red's marks were brimming with power and that could have attracted the shadow's attention. We'd learned a few years ago with Ember that even if the shadow's hunger was satiated a strong sexual desire could reignite a glimmer of its hunger.

Perhaps Ember, with her need to find the rest of her mates, along with Red's overwhelming desire, had been enough to partially reawaken it.

My cock stirred at the thought.

Shit.

Shit shit shit. Focus, damn it.

It didn't matter what had happened last night. That shouldn't have affected the shadow's allure this afternoon. Given how much Quill said Talon had consumed from the boy, he shouldn't have been radiating any allure for the rest of the rotation.

Unless, of course, like Talon suspected, there was something unusual about Sawyer Herstind.

"Once around the trail," Rider barked, not waiting for Talon and Quill to reach us, his wolf deepening his voice as he watched Sawyer get more and more uncomfortable. "Last one runs again at the end of training with the bag of rocks."

Tyon, the chef's assistant who'd been the slowest last time, sighed, knowing Mikel and Durand weren't going to be dumb enough to talk back to Rider and save him from the extra round this time.

Boy, was he going to be pleasantly surprised to find out he wasn't last and Sawyer really was behind him this time.

The group took off down the trail with most of the fae novices leading the pack, their naturally-faster-than-human speed and their longer legs making it easy for them to run past most of the humans.

Sawyer, having learned from the previous few times where we'd bumped and tripped him at the beginning of the trail, let all but the slowest novices run ahead of him, forcing Bramwell to stop out of sight of Rider and pretend to retie his boots so the boy would pass him.

It was a risk putting Bramwell behind him, since Sawyer was normally faster than him and he might fall too far behind, but Sawyer would suspect something was up if it was anyone else. Mikel guessed that Sawyer would pace himself to keep his distance ahead of Bramwell, not letting him catch up, but not put on any extra speed to catch up to us, and he was right.

The boy was still out of sight behind us when Durand and I ran around the sharp turn in the path and into the clearing. Ahead lay the log spanning the waist-deep stream with tall, sheer banks on either side.

This part of the trail tested balance or teamwork depending on if you could make it across the log or not. For the fae and those of us who were almost as tall as the fae, a good jump from the river and we could grab the ledge and haul ourselves up, but for everyone else — unless they were expert climbers and could find foot and handholds in the almost sheer rockface — they'd need help climbing up.

Mikel and Hamelin had already crossed the log — and given that they were dry, they'd managed to keep their balance or straddled the log to make their way across. Behind us, the last two fae novices rounded the bend and gave us strange looks as we let them cross.

They had to know something was up and would likely figure out what when Sawyer ran into the practice area last, dripping wet, but I doubted they'd say anything to Rider. Getting wet and running the course again was nothing compared to the punishment most of the Guardsmen thought Sawyer deserved.

Then Sawyer strode into sight as if he'd already figured out he was walking into a trap. The thought sent a flicker of pride swelling through me. He was smart and observant and if novice training didn't break him, he was a possible candidate for my Shadow Guard.

Of course, that all depended on if he could handle

spying on and assassinating the enemies of the Realms. Not everyone had the stomach for the kind of duties I required of my men, no matter how noble the cause, and most of the Guardsmen didn't have the wit, perception, or forethought to survive.

"So this is the plan," he said, his gaze darting over us, his expression wary.

Mikel pointed to the stream. "You get in or we throw you in."

Sawyer's gaze flickered to the steep bank at Mikel's feet then to the log. He knew the bank was too tall and he also knew that the odds were slim that anyone behind us would offer him a hand out. He also knew even if he made it across the log, he would be in for one hell of a fight against Mikel and Hamelin. So what would he choose?

A part of me wanted to see him fight, just to see how far he could get. He was out-numbered and far too small to take even two of us in a fight, but he was quick. If he got past Mikel and Hamelin, he might make it to the end of the trail before we caught him.

But before he could make his decision, Bramwell raced around the corner behind him. He saw Sawyer standing half between him and the edge of the stream and he put on a burst of speed and rushed at the boy.

Sawyer side-stepped out of the way at the last second, the movement fluid, almost fae-like, and gave the bigger man a shove that wouldn't have done much of anything if Bramwell had been standing still.

But the push, along with his momentum, sent Bramwell staggering forward and he tumbled over the edge before he could stop himself.

"Big mistake, runt," Durand snapped and he lunged for Sawyer.

Sawyer darted out of the way and dashed toward the log bridge. Durand was almost as fast as he was but bigger and stronger and if Durand caught him the fight would be over.

I really wanted to let him go, see if he could actually make it across the log without falling, but that would piss off Mikel and I couldn't afford to be ousted from the group, so I jumped in Sawyer's way, cutting him off from the bridge.

With a yell, Duran dove for him and he tried to doge Durand's grasp but wasn't fast enough. Durand seized the back of his jerkin, yanked him off his feet, and slammed him onto the ground.

Sawyer hit hard, his breath exploded from his body and his face tightened in pain, but he fought through it instead of drawing in on himself like he had during the sparring session with Rider and attempted to twist and punch his way out of Durand's grip.

His knuckles skimmed Durand's chin, drawing a snarl and a retaliatory punch that landed solidly on the boy's cheek, and his head jerked to the side.

Durand followed with another powerful punch into the boy's chest. Sawyer gasped, fighting to catch his breath as Durand hauled him to the bank and jumped in, taking the boy with him.

"Learn your lesson," he snarled, shoving Sawyer's head under the water.

Sawyer flailed and heaved against Durand's grip but couldn't break free. Durand yanked him up, letting him gasp in a partial breath then shoved his head back under.

"Learn your fucking lesson."

Another wrench up, another gasping breath, and the boy's head was back under water.

Fuck. It didn't look like Durand was going to stop, and from the looks of everyone else, no one was going to speak up and stop him.

"Durand, enough," I yelled.

"You're not better than me," Durand sneered at Sawyer even though he couldn't hear him. "You're not better than any of us."

"Durand." I jumped into the stream, the cold water instantly soaking my pants all the way up to my hips. I yanked Sawyer out of Durand's grip and shoved Durand back. He lost his balance and fell, slipping under the water and coming up sputtering, his eyes filled with deadly rage.

"Kill him and the Lord Commander will kill you," I snapped at him as Sawyer gasped and trembled in my grip, reminding me of another redhead's trembling and gasping. *Fuck. Focus.* "You saw his claws yesterday. He's a fucking animal."

"He's right," Mikel said, crouching on the bank and offering Durand a hand up. "Don't waste your life on the runt."

"I'm dead anyway if I have to depend on him to watch my back," Durand snarled.

Mikel glanced at Sawyer, who wrenched out of my grip and staggered back. He still gasped for breath, and hurt and fear filled his eyes.

For a moment I was overwhelmed with the sense to protect him, just like I'd been overwhelmed to protect Red when Wells and Crane had stepped into the courtyard. She'd been terrified of them — still was — and now Sawyer was terrified of us. The look twisted in my chest. I needed to protect her— *him, damn it. Him.*

Fuck. I wanted to protect both of them.

Neither of them deserved to be afraid, and while I could tell Rider what happened to Sawyer, I really couldn't afford to lose Mikel's trust. Now more than ever I needed to stay close to him so I could at the very least control the damage from the next attack, since Durand seemed intent on killing him and Mikel intent on letting it happen.

This was one of the parts of my job that I hated. I was going to stand back and watch while these men beat up a boy and not do anything about it unless it looked like they were actually going to kill him or he was going to give up and kill himself.

Then the fear in Sawyer's eyes hardened into determination edged with anger and he turned away and sloshed upstream through the waist-high water — that was almost chest-high on the boy — in search of a way out.

My fear for him shifted into a strange mix of relief and pride. I didn't think the boy would try to pay Mikel back for what just happened, but he wasn't going to lie down and take whatever was thrown at him next. He was going to make the bastards work for it.

"Do you think he's going to tell the Lord Commander?" Bramwell asked as he grabbed the top of the bank and hauled himself out. The big man almost looked sorry for what had happened, while Hamelin, standing beside him, looked downright concerned.

"He won't," Mikel said with a satisfied smirk as he watched Sawyer half walk half swim around a bend in the stream and disappear from sight. "He knows it'll be worse if he goes crying to Rider and then it won't just be us reminding him of his place. It'll be everyone."

I nodded my agreement and forced a smirk, but I hated that Mikel was right.

Sawyer was smart enough to know going to Rider for help right now would only make his situation worse with the other men. Reporting on one attack that ended up with him wet and running the course again would make him look weak and spoiled, and Sawyer was smart enough to realize looking weak or spoiled wouldn't help him here.

That, and the boy was too stubborn for his own good. From what Quill had told me about how he'd tried to run the trail even after Talon's shadow had attacked him, I doubted Sawyer would ask for help even if Durand had beaten him unconscious.

Which meant I couldn't afford to be distracted. One slip up and the boy could be seriously hurt or killed. I had to stop thinking about Red. Sawyer's life depended on it.

CHAPTER 28
Sage

I WADED UP STREAM, still struggling to catch my breath. My cheek stung and my chest throbbed where Durand had hit me and I couldn't stop shaking, but I kept pushing forward.

It didn't matter how far I had to go to find a way out of the ravine, and there was no point in turning back in the hope that one of my fellow novices would offer me a hand up.

They wouldn't. No one would.

Even after Durand and Mikel and the rest of those guys left, the other novices wouldn't help me. They'd already made that perfectly clear.

A shudder swept through me and my stomach clenched tight.

Durand had almost killed me and Mikel had watched with a gleeful grin that was far too similar to

Pylos's when Edred had been beating me or Sawyer. But worse were Bramwell and Hamelin. They had at least looked a little uncomfortable, but hadn't tried to stop him, while Ambrose—

I had no idea what to make of Ambrose.

He'd saved me, but he hadn't looked as uneasy as Bramwell or Hamelin had about Durand's attack. His expression had been hard, and he'd barely given me a second glance after he'd pulled Durand off me, as if it hadn't been me he'd been trying to save, but Durand. And yet... there was something about Ambrose that I couldn't quite place, like he wasn't all that he seemed to be.

Maybe he was one of the men from my vision who was going to kill me.

But the moment I thought that, I just knew he wasn't.

Except I couldn't say exactly how I knew. I just did.

Besides, even if he wasn't responsible for my impending death, I doubted he'd help me. Any aid I got from him would be because he was trying to save his friends from Lord Rider's wrath.

And really, I just needed to hold on for four and a half, maybe five, more rotations. Just keep my head down and take it. I certainly couldn't complain about it. Complaining would only make things worse.

But the idea of just taking it made me want to

scream, even if I knew that taking whatever they threw at me meant protecting Sawyer.

Except Sawyer wouldn't be safe if one of them killed me before he was out of the Great Five Kingdoms, and I had to admit, it had been satisfying to watch Bramwell fall into the stream, not to mention the look on Durand's face when I'd almost landed that punch.

Of course, then I'd seen stars when he'd hit me and not much of anything when he'd shoved my head under water. I hadn't even thought to draw my weapons... although I had a feeling if I had, Durand wouldn't have had a problem stabbing me with his and he was the stronger fighter in every way. There was no way I'd win a fight against him, with or without weapons.

I slapped the water and swallowed back a scream. I didn't think they'd followed me, but I didn't want them to know how frustrated I was.

Why couldn't they just leave me alone? Ignore me, give me the cold shoulder, pretend I didn't exist, and deny me oranges. I could survive that. My *disguise* could survive that.

But attacking me? Now I was completely soaked and had a bruise on my cheek and it hurt even more when I breathed. How was I going to explain that without Lord Quill or Talon telling me to go to the infirmary? Hell, given how Lord Rider had reacted yesterday when Talon's shadow had attacked me, he'd probably tell me to go, too.

A shudder of desire teased down my spine at the thought of Talon's magic. It was a whisper of what it had been yesterday, and I was grateful for my last night with Fantasy Man because I was pretty sure having sex with him had helped, but I still remembered what it felt like. I didn't think I'd ever forget.

The memory of his magic had swelled inside me and my breath had stalled the minute I'd seen Talon and Lord Quill jogging across the practice yard toward me. I had no idea how I was going to face them — hell, face anyone — once I found a way out of this ravine.

Four and a half rotations. Four and a half damned rotations. That's all I needed and then I could beg for Lord Rider's forgiveness.

But only if the vision of my impending death didn't come to pass first.

I dragged my gaze over the steep bank.

If I stood on my toes, I could probably get my fingers over the rocky edge just like I could with the bank by the log bridge, but there still weren't any good footholds and I certainly didn't have the strength to haul myself up even if I jumped and managed to get a better grip.

There are a lot of things I don't have the strength for, I thought bitterly.

I couldn't stop looking at Lord Quill or Talon or

even Lord Rider, and I didn't stand a chance in a fight against Durand, Mikel, Bramwell, Hamelin, or Ambrose.

I swore to myself when I'd had the vision of those men standing over my body that I'd become stronger, be a better fighter, but I didn't have any extra time for training, and it felt like my body was going to hurt forever.

Now, with Kit, Payne, and Lewin on night shift, it was obvious there wasn't anyone who'd teach me, so even if I did stop hurting and found some free time, I wasn't going to get additional training.

Of course, from the looks on Durand and Mikel's faces, they weren't going to stop with that one attack at the bridge. They were going to come at me hard during sparring and probably ambush me again on the trail.

I was going to get extra fighting experience whether I wanted to or not and — Great Father this was a terrible idea — if I acted more like a haughty lord, they probably wouldn't wait a few days before their next attempt. I could get extra training every day if I just made them think I wasn't learning their lesson of humility.

It was an extremely dangerous game, one I didn't want to play. There was a chance they'd break something and I'd be forced to go to the infirmary, and that would be the end of everything.

But maybe a small lie about how Rider would seriously punish them if they sent someone to the infirmary would be enough for Durand and Mikel to watch how aggressive they were. Or, at the very least, for Bramwell, Hamelin, and Ambrose to stop them before things got out of hand.

I'd have to tell the lie to the other novices. I couldn't just tell Mikel and his group. They wouldn't believe me. But if they heard it from the others...

Hell, they already thought I was getting special treatment. I could play that up a bit, make them think I really was getting special treatment. That would increase the likelihood of them attacking me but also make them wary of hurting me too badly.

I had no doubt the other novices would tell each other. Half the Guard had known I was the one who'd come through the fae ring after dark by breakfast the next day. I doubted the novices gossiped less than the rest of the Guard.

The real question was who did I say it to? Tyon maybe? He was around my age — my real age — and the shyest among the novices. He also could use a hand up.

If I suggested he make friends with Talon or Lord Quill and that they'd talk to Rider about treating him better than everyone else, he might mention that to his friends. I didn't know if he had friends at the Black Tower, but he wasn't me, so the other novices probably weren't ignoring him like they were me.

With my new terrible plan firmly in mind, I pushed through the waist-high water until the bank on my right was lower than my shoulders.

There still weren't any good places to get a foothold, but the bank's height remained level as far as I could see and I couldn't afford to waste any more time. I might want to piss off the other novices into inadvertently giving me more fighting experience, but I didn't want to piss off Lord Rider, or at least piss him off any more than I already was— alright fine, any more than my 'special treatment' lie would.

Gritting my teeth, I grabbed the edge of the bank and jumped as high as I could. The top half of my chest hit the hard edge, sending agony screaming through me, and I fought through the pain, my toes uselessly scrabbling against the sheer rock wall, and somehow managed to haul myself up onto the bank.

Darkness flickered across my vision, and I rolled onto my back to catch my breath, each rapid inhalation shooting more pain through me.

Above me, mist curled through the scraggly tree branches as if a cloud had sunk and skimmed the earth, and a hint of a shadow lazily drifted through the mist overhead like a bird circling its prey.

The sight sent a shiver through me, chilling my wet skin. I knew next to nothing about the shadow monsters that inhabited the Gray, hadn't really thought of them since being attacked my first night here, but there was a chance I was going to have to face them before my four and a half rotations were up.

That thought just added to the worries weighing inside me: protect Sawyer, avoid being murdered, try not to get beaten up too badly, and fight the monsters hiding in the mist.

Sure. No problem.

The shadow circled closer, getting bigger and bigger and bigger, until its large claws — claws that were bigger than my head — skimmed the top of the scraggly trees above me.

My pulse stuttered. It was enormous, twice the size of a horse, and looked like the drawing of the dragon in the book of legendary creatures Sawyer had found in the castle library. The only thing that made it different from the dragon in the book were the whisps of black miasma undulating around its body.

With a screech, it folded its massive leathery wings back and dove for me.

Oh, shadows! It *was* a dragon!

I scrambled to my feet and bolted along the bank back to the running trail. The trail was magically protected from the shadows during the daytime — but not at night, since the shadows were too strong after sunset — but it looked like not *all* of the area around the trail was covered.

The shadow dragon's claws scraped against the hard ground where I'd been lying, and it swung its large, reptilian head toward me and snapped at me with teeth that were as big and long as Payne's enormous broadswords.

With a grunt, I jerked out of the way, feeling the wind of its movement at my back. I ran away from the bank before I fell back into the ravine, crashing into the underbrush where the trees were closer together and hoping that would make it harder to get me.

The dragon screeched and a blast of frozen breath gusted over me, partially freezing the water in my clothes and hair.

Oh shadows oh shadows oh shadows.

I jerked around another tree trunk, slammed my shin against a protruding rock, stumbled, but managed to keep my balance and kept going while the monster crashed through the underbrush after me.

I forced myself to move faster, my arms up in front of my face to protect it against the tree branches, then something *cracked* sharply behind me.

A large tree tumbled to the ground with a heavy *thud*, narrowly missing me, then another and another as the monster barreled toward me, the trees no longer an obstacle.

Oh, fuck. So much for hoping that would slow it down.

I leaped over a fallen log, wrenched to the side before doing more damage to my shins against another rock, and drew my sword.

The best plan was to find a hole small enough to hide in where it couldn't reach me, but I couldn't see anything like that.

I really didn't want to fight it. I didn't stand a chance against it, but I had no idea how far away I was from the trail or if the trail would even protect me from it.

With a snarl, it snapped its jaws at me. Its teeth grazed the back of my head as its breath turned the water in my hair into a heavy chunk of ice, and my pulse stuttered.

Please, Father save me!

I swung wildly behind me. The tip of my blade nicked the inside edge of one of its nostrils, but that only pissed it off.

It roared another blast of frozen breath over me that stiffened my clothes and made me stumble. My toe hit a bump in the ground, and I fell, my momentum tumbling me forward, head over heels, until I crashed into another tree.

The world spun around me, speckled with flashes of light and darkness. The monster screeched and started to snap at me again but jerked back as if stung. It hissed and tried to eat me again, but always pulled back before reaching me as if something was stopping it.

No, not something. The magical protection on the trail.

I crawled farther away, not wanting to test the protection against the shadow monster's determination, until my shaky limbs couldn't hold me, and I collapsed, gasping and trembling from fear and cold, and curled into a ball.

Tears pricked my eyes, and I fought them but couldn't stop them. The emotion roaring inside me needed to come out somehow, and I hurt and couldn't breathe and was exhausted and almost died twice in the last hour… hell, probably the last thirty minutes.

I couldn't do this. I couldn't fight shadow monsters and horrible men and everything else. I was just a girl. I wasn't a swordsman and I was never going to be a swordmaiden.

Except I'd already learned there wasn't anything *just* about being a girl. I was a better swordsman than half the novices here, I'd already killed a shadow monster — even if it had been by accident — and I knew I could get even better.

I was strong, not just because I needed to protect my brother, but because I *was* strong in spirit, plain and simple. I had a plan to become a better swordsman — swords*woman* and I'd be damned if I would give up now.

I was in this until I was found out. And maybe by the time that happened, I'd know enough to defend myself against Edred and any other man who wanted to put me in my place.

CHAPTER 29
Rider

SAWYER WAS LATE. Tyon had run off the trail, huffing, trying to catch his breath, and the boy was nowhere in sight. He should have arrived before Bramwell, but the large novice and his group of friends had arrived minutes ago, Mikel with a smug smile, and Bramwell, Durand, and Ambrose soaking wet. And while Bramwell had fallen off the log bridge before, Durand and Ambrose hadn't, which made me suspect they'd ambushed Sawyer at the stream.

I'd expected them to attempt something like that and also for the other novices to not help the boy out of the stream, but even if he'd hiked to where the bank was low enough for him to climb out, he should have been back by now... unless he'd just given up and hadn't bothered trying to hurry back.

Except I knew that wasn't true. So far, the boy

hadn't given up and I doubted being forced to find a way out of the ravine would stop him.

Which meant something else had gone wrong and if they'd seriously hurt him, I wasn't going to be able to keep my wolf at bay. I needed everybody I had right now protecting the Gray, even small bodies like Sawyer's.

And the second I thought that, a shadow dragon's screech cut through the misty air. Talon and Quill shot me worried looks, obviously realizing like I had that Sawyer had been forced off the trail. And while most of the area around the trail was safe — and should have been safe from shadow dragons since they never came this close to the Tower — Sawyer was particularly short and would have had to go farther up or down stream to find a way out of the ravine.

The creature shrieked again, followed by numerous heavy thuds, and off in the distance the mist undulated and swirled as if something large had disturbed it, the sign that the shadow dragon had found something and was really going after it.

And that *it* could only be Sawyer Herstind.

Fuck. I'd finally managed to calm myself down from Talon's attack on Sawyer and now the boy was being chased down by a shadow dragon that shouldn't have even been around to notice him.

Because of course it had to be after Sawyer. The

boy had the worst luck — or the best depending on how you looked at it.

This was not how I wanted my day to go.

"Quill, take the novices who have no experience with daggers and show them the basics. Talon, you've got the fae and the experienced humans," I barked, catching the eyes of Slate, Zorin, and Jalnar, the three closest Guardsmen doing their afternoon training on the other side of the novice's training area. "You three with me."

I turned and ran, not waiting for my men. They'd catch up soon enough, and right now, every second counted.

Out of the corner of my eye I saw Hamelin shoot Ambrose a worried look, while Mikel and Durand looked put out, like saving the boy's ass was giving him special treatment or something when they were the ones who'd put him in danger in the first place.

Fucking idiots.

They hadn't even been here for a rotation, and they were already getting on my nerves. Why couldn't they just leave the boy alone and learn their fucking job?

But their job depended on Sawyer learning his job, and they, along with the other Guardsmen feared that Sawyer was too selfish and too weak to watch their backs.

It was like they'd all forgotten that the boy had already killed a hound.

Of course, Mikel and his group probably thought that was an exaggeration. That it was me, Talon, and Quill giving him more special attention, and I couldn't dispute that without looking like I was favoring Sawyer.

The shadow dragon screeched again, and I barreled down the hill at the trail's end and into the cover of the trees. The log bridge was just after the halfway point, and with a shadow dragon every second counted. If I went the wrong way, I could be too late.

Goddess damned fucking idiots.

If the boy died, they were going to be on stable duty and laundry duty and the dirtiest, hardest jobs I could find for the rest of their fucking lives. Which I knew wasn't realistic because I needed them on the wall and securing the land around the Tower, but damn it! It had been years since I'd lost a Guardsman to the sheer stupidity of other Guardsmen, and I sure as hell didn't want to lose one now.

I raced around the bend, my wolf straining to tear out of my body, eager for a fight and to release the frustration that had been building inside me from the moment Sawyer had come through the ring after dark and painted a target on his pathetically small chest.

What the hell was wrong with this group of novices?

The shadow dragon released a bellowing roar, sending a wave of cold air sweeping out of the scraggly forest and chilling my skin. It rose above me, an enormous monster that even I would have trouble taking down by myself in my wolf form, and shook it's head as if it had bumped it... or as if it had caught something, a predator shaking its prey into submission.

My stomach bottomed out as it flew away, and I gritted my teeth, pushing to run faster. There might not be a body, but I had to look anyway. If he was alive and injured, I had to get him to the infirmary. If he was dead and left behind, I couldn't leave him rotting in the Gray. No one deserved that.

From where the shadow dragon had risen out of the trees, it had to have been at the edge of the barrier close to the log bridge.

I cut off the trail, heading to the edge of the barrier to follow it around to the stream, my senses on high alert. Just because the shadow dragon had flown away, didn't mean it wouldn't come back, or that smaller opportunistic shadows hoping for scraps off whatever the shadow dragon left behind wouldn't show up... not that shadow dragons usually left much behind when they attacked a human.

Hell, Sawyer was so small, he probably wasn't even a satisfying snack.

I rounded a large chunk of rock jutting out from the ground to see the boy lying on his back just inside the barrier protecting the trail. His palms were pressed against his eyes and his chest heaved with desperate breaths. Water and flecks of ice pooled around him, giving evidence to my theory that he'd ended up in the stream, and a hint of blood, that my wolf senses noticed, tinted the pool by his right foot, making my wolf snarl inside me. He'd ripped his pants again, the tear exposing a bleeding gash in his shin and the swelling and purpling of what was going to be a painful bruise.

I purposefully stepped on a dry twig, making it crack, and he shot upright, his eyes wide. He reached for his sword, making me smile inwardly at the instinct. But his sheath was empty, the blade lying a few feet from him, so he quickly switched to grab his dagger before his wild eyes landed on me.

CHAPTER 30
Rider

"OH, THANK THE FATHER," he groaned, his gaze sliding over the rocky ground around him, but I couldn't tell if he was actually seeing anything or not.

He hadn't pissed himself when he'd faced off against a pack of shadow hounds, nor when he'd had to stand his ground and spar with me, but a shadow dragon was a whole other kind of monster. He had to be in shock.

I bit back a growl.

Twice in as many days. How much more could the boy take?

And while yes, eventually he was going to have to face the shadows in the Gray, I usually didn't start the novices off with hounds and dragons and never alone. Even after the novices became full Guardsmen, they never fought shadows, big or small, alone. I was the only idiot who did that, and only when my wolf's nature overwhelmed my common sense.

Then his attention landed on his sword and the realization of how ridiculous it was that he'd drawn it hit me. Drawing meant he'd intended to use it, which, unless he knew exactly where to strike, had been completely pointless. Surely, he'd known just looking at the thing that his tiny blade didn't stand a chance.

"Were you stupid enough to think you could fight it?" I huffed.

"No, I was going to offer to pick its teeth," he drawled.

Holy shit.

I stared at him, stunned. Had he just made a joke?

His eyes widened with horror as his brain caught up to his mouth.

"Oh, my goodness! I'm so sorry, my lord. I didn't mean— I thought—" He slapped his hands over his lips to physically stop himself from talking.

I burst into laughter. It was highly inappropriate. A commander was supposed to be tough and in control at all times, but I couldn't stop myself. I knew he had a bright spark and had been hiding it. Guess it just took one hell of a shock to break past his walls.

"I didn't know where the barrier was and didn't have many options. Running into the trees didn't even slow it down." He rolled to his hands and knees, realized he'd hurt his shin and that crawling was a bad idea, so he tried to stand instead.

Jeez. Really? "Sit," I snarled. "You're going to crack your skull open."

Slate and Jalnar rushed around the rocks, weapons drawn even though they'd seen the shadow dragon fly away like I had. I didn't see Zorin, but knew he was just behind them, watching their backs, keeping an eye out for scavengers even though we were inside the barrier.

"It didn't break through the barrier so we're good," I told them. "I've got the novice. You're dismissed."

Jalnar's dark gaze dipped to Sawyer and he frowned, but I couldn't tell if he was seeing the boy in a new light — the light I'd seen him in once I'd realized he'd actually tried to stand his ground against that pack of hounds — or not.

Slate gave me a tight nod, his expression also hard to read as he and Jalnar marched back to the trail. He, at least, was friends with Kit and Payne. If I hadn't needed to keep the hunting teams half human and half fae, he would have been a good addition to their unit. The three of them worked well together. Maybe my cousin and his mate had said something to convince Slate to see what they saw in the boy.

Or maybe I was just hoping for that. Everything would be easier for me and hence easier for Sawyer if the other Guardsmen just got over themselves and got back to the business of defending the Gray.

Fuck. I'd never felt fully comfortable as Lord Commander, but since Sawyer's arrival, it felt like I was the worst person for the job.

I grabbed the boy's sword and knelt in front of him to check the cut on his leg before he could stand again. He was pale, but not as pale as he'd been yesterday so he probably hadn't hit his head, and from the amount of blood in the water around him, it looked like he'd managed to get away with just the gash on his leg and some scrapes and bruises.

With a huff, I straightened and offered him a hand to help him stand. "Can you walk?"

"Yes, my lord." He grabbed his sword, wiped shadow blood from the tip onto his pantleg — which surprised the hell out of me because it meant he'd actually struck the shadow dragon — and sheathed his weapon.

"I want you to get Flint to dress that," I ordered. "And unless he puts you on bed rest, you change your pants and get back to the practice yard."

Any other novice I'd tell him to stay with Flint so the healer could watch him. With Sawyer's inexperience, the reality of how close he'd been to losing his life could hit him hard, and it was best if someone better able to deal with *feelings* was there when reality sunk in.

But the other novices had already started his unsanctioned training and giving him yet another afternoon off would only make things worse for him. And as much as I hated it, having Sawyer tough it out and earn the other Guardsmen's respect was the best way out of this mess for everyone.

"Yes, my lord."

We crested the last hill, and I marched back to the practice area while Sawyer half jogged, half hobbled to the pasture gate.

Everyone watched us as we approached, the novices with a mix of fear and disgust and the other Guardsmen in the practice area with curiosity and wariness.

Quill raised an eyebrow in a silent question that I didn't want to answer with everyone around, and Talon watched the boy as if he couldn't tear his gaze away from him.

"Back to work," I barked and everyone jerked their attention away from Sawyer. "Talon, take the fae. The humans in your group are mine."

Talon's group split, the fae novices going to a third sparring circle, and I glared at the remaining humans. Mikel, Durand, Ambrose, and Hamelin met my gaze head on as if daring me to call them out over what had happened. Bramwell looked concerned, his gaze kept flickering between me and Sawyer, while Sivis, Aldis, and Jokin stood at attention their eyes a little too wide, likely from the shadow dragon's screeches.

"What the hell was that?" one of the novices in

Talon's group whispered. Their backs were turned to me, and I wasn't familiar enough with their voices to identify him, so I wasn't entirely sure who'd spoken.

"Don't know, but it sounded big," someone else replied.

I heaved my attention back to my novices. "Mikel. Jokin. In the ring. You know the rules."

The men each grabbed a practice dagger and started circling each other, looking for an opportunity to strike.

"Did you see the runt?" someone whispered. This from Quill's group. Swell, even the inexperienced novices were referring to him as the runt.

"The Lord Commander ran awfully fast to save him," another man huffed.

"Yeah well, you heard what I heard," a third replied. "If whatever that was came after me, I'd want the Lord Commander to come running, too."

Jokin lunged toward Mikel, and again I had to force myself to concentrate on their fight. The points with daggers were often quick and partially hidden, and I had to pay attention and stop trying to overhear what the other men thought of my smallest, trouble-magnet novice. Ash would keep me informed on how the novices were getting along, and if things became dire, he'd reveal himself and stop whatever was going on.

Sawyer returned from the infirmary faster than I would have expected — guess the shock of almost being eaten by a shadow dragon hadn't sunk in yet — and I waved him over to join our group.

The rest of training went surprisingly smoothly, although I made sure Sawyer's three fights were with Aldis, Jokin, and Sivis, men who I was pretty sure hadn't been involved with forcing Sawyer into the stream.

Then the seventh bell rang and all of the novices' eyes darted to the bags of rocks still sitting by the mouth of the trail.

I bit back a sigh knowing what they were all thinking. If Sawyer was well enough to train, he was well enough to take the punishment of finishing last. "Sawyer. One lap around the trail."

The boy picked up a bag of rocks without complaint, slung it over his shoulder, and strode — still limping a bit — over the hill.

Mikel turned toward the Tower but not before I saw his smirk and the knowing look that passed between him and Durand. Then a similar, if slightly worried, look passed between the other three, but I wasn't sure if that meant they were satisfied with Sawyer's punishment or not.

Talon waited until the novices were on their way back to the Tower before giving me a sharp look, likely about to argue with me for sending an injured Sawyer to run the trail where he'd almost been killed. But

Quill grabbed his arm and tugged him toward the Tower.

"We'll talk about it in the Garden with Ash," Quill said. "No point in repeating ourselves."

"No." Talon jerked back around to face me. "How close did the shadow dragon get to him?"

"Too close, and no, we're not talking about it until we're with Ash. Quill, you should be here when he finishes his run." I grabbed the second bag of rocks and hefted it onto my shoulder. "He doesn't know where to return the rocks and the whole shadow dragon thing probably hasn't hit him yet."

"You think he's going to fall apart?" Quill asked.

Would he? The second thing the boy had said to me had been a joke... so probably not. At least not without a whole lot more heaped on those narrow shoulders of his. "I don't think so. Not yet. But just in case, you're better at handling that stuff than I am."

Talon would have been the best choice, but I still wasn't sure if it was safe to leave those two alone together. Sure, his shadow hadn't made an appearance and Sawyer hadn't been so overwhelmed by Talon's allure that he couldn't concentrate this afternoon, but they'd still ended up staring at each other, looking like they were trying not to look and unable to help themselves.

And the more I thought about it, the more it seemed the situation wasn't because something in

Talon's shadow had changed, but because there was something about Sawyer Herstind.

My pulse skipped a beat. The hounds could have been explained by him coming through the ring after dark, but the shadow dragon shouldn't have been near the Tower, especially during the day, and Talon's shadow had attacked the boy in a way I'd never seen before.

Could there be something about Sawyer Herstind, about his fae-touched magical nature, that attracted shadows?

And if so, that was the worst possible trait a Guardsman could have... or the best if he was willing to use himself as bait.

CHAPTER 31
Talon

True to his word Rider refused to talk to me about Sawyer and the novices as we headed back to the Tower. We grabbed some food from the kitchen but parted ways on the top floor of the Tower to go to our separate rooms. Rider had a meeting with his seneschal to go over the latest supply orders, and I had a fresh set of reports from Ash's Shadow Guard about what the nobility were doing in the Gold Tower that I needed to look at.

Strangely, my shadow was quiet, content to rest under my skin, woven through — or rather trapped in — my magical ability to control darkness. It had been excited to see Sawyer standing by the trail's entrance and had been as relieved as I was that we hadn't seriously hurt him after feeding on him yesterday.

But even as excited as it was — which made it hard

for me to look away — it kept a tight hold on its allure, knowing it was far too soon to feed on the boy again.

At least until the shadow dragon had screeched and we'd realized the beast had to have been after Sawyer. Then it had tried to explode from my body, take control, and save him.

It had taken everything I had to obey Rider's orders and start the afternoon training while he, Slate, Zorin, and Jalnar had rushed off, and while my shadow had relaxed the moment Sawyer had hobbled into sight, the rest of me still churned with frustration that Rider had commanded Sawyer to return to training after Flint had dressed his wound.

And that frustration had turned to anger when he'd told Sawyer to run the trail again.

I closed my eyes and sent my spirit to the Garden, choosing to appear a few feet from the three benches just outside the courtyard where we were supposed to meet.

Rider sat alone, his attention focused over his shoulder across the manicured lawn and flowerbeds to a small pool that sat near the main path to the courtyard. The space around it was empty, the small stone bench an invitation for solitary meditation or a very intimate conversation, and I had no idea why he was so intent on it.

Maybe he'd seen a rabbit or something and his wolf was straining for control. I had no doubt he was just as pissed as I was about the afternoon, just for different reasons.

Black smoke swirled into the space beside me, and Quill's spirit form manifested. He wore a green and gold jerkin instead of his black Guardsman uniform like Rider and I did, the colors accentuating his green eyes and golden hair.

My breath stalled even as my shadow undulated under my skin. After feeding on Sawyer and Quill yesterday it was satisfied — more or less — but it felt my love for Quill and sympathized with my heartache over never being able to bond with him.

Of course, it was also confused as to why I refused to bond with him since that was what I desperately wanted, because it didn't understand the complex emotion of loving someone so deeply you'd sacrifice your desires to see them happy.

"What are you looking at?" Quill asked as he sat on the bench across from Rider.

Rider jerked his attention away from the pool and ran his hand through his hair. A few strands fell out of his topknot and framed his face, drawing my attention to the exhaustion in his silver eyes and reminding me that I wasn't the only one struggling right now.

"Nothing," he replied, his voice gruff.

Quill raised an eyebrow at that, but I wasn't sure at what. Rider didn't usually stare at nothing, but with everything going on at the Black Tower it wouldn't have surprised me if he'd just been lost in thought trying to figure out how to turn our current group of novices into a team and get them into a full rotation as quickly as possible.

Someone barked a hearty laugh inside the courtyard, the green curtains hiding whoever it was from view.

The mood in the Garden had become brighter, louder, and more hopeful since the arrival of the new, redhaired woman a few nights ago. Everyone was eager to meet her, court her, hell, just help her ease the building sexual pressure from her mating marks.

Even if they didn't have magic and knew they'd never be mated, she was another chance for them to be with a fae woman.

Everyone except Quill.

He didn't just want a little sex. He wanted a mate and children, and every time a new woman showed up he got hopeful... and then disappointed, which broke my heart a little more each time.

Three men stepped out of the courtyard, one of them gesticulating wildly, telling a story that the other men were laughing at. The man on his right elbowed him and jerked his chin at Rider and all three of them shared a strange, knowing look, the kind of look the Guardsmen gave each other in Lehyrst when they managed to score one of the prettier, or more talented, pleasure house girls.

Quill quirked an eyebrow and glanced at me, but I had no idea what it meant. Whatever it was, I doubted it was true. Rider had been abstinent since his human wife had died so the look mustn't have been what I thought it was. Which only made me wonder what else it could have been.

But before I could figure it out, Ash materialized on the other side of the benches. He was dressed all in black — although not his Guardsman uniform — with his jaw-length dark-brown hair hanging lose, partially hiding the ugly red scar marring the right side of his face. His obsidian gaze darted around us as if he was looking for someone, his body tense, before he realized what he was doing and his posture and demeanor snapped to his usual, in-control calm.

"We need to make this quick," he said, dropping onto the third, unoccupied bench in our seating area.

"Worried Mikel and his group will try something tonight?" Quill asked as I sat beside him.

"I'm not sure." His attention danced past Rider's shoulder, back to looking for someone for a second, then jumped back to us. "It helped that Sawyer came back to training and you made him run the trail again, but I'm concerned about how far Durand and Mikel are willing to go."

"And I'm concerned you pushed him too hard today," I said, Ash reminding me that I was pissed at Rider for making the boy run while injured.

"He's not a child," Rider snapped, his gaze starting to shift back to the pool before he ran his hands through his hair, stopping his head from turning, and glared at me. "Flint didn't keep him or put him on bedrest, so he couldn't have been hurt that badly."

"I'd beg to differ on the child part," I said, meeting Rider's glare, my shadow writhing over my hands and arms.

Quill grabbed my hand and the pressure and smoke from my shadow eased, its writhing softening into a gentle caress over our skin. "He's fine. His limp was a little more pronounced once he'd finished running with the rocks, but he didn't look upset about going past the place where he'd been attacked by the shadow dragon."

"Maybe he wasn't attacked and didn't see it," Ash suggested. "Maybe it went after something else and the boy was just nearby."

"Nope, he saw it," Rider said. "He had shadow blood on the tip of his sword."

"Well, shit," Ash huffed. "The boy's got a target tattooed on his forehead or something. He managed to piss off Durand enough to make him snap and almost drown him."

"Drown him? Durand almost drowned him?" I jerked forward, my shadow suddenly furious, lashing at the air around me despite Quill's calming presence *and* the fact that I was in my spirit form where my shadow should have been weaker.

"What the hell?" Ash hissed, jerking back to avoid a slashing tendril, his eyes wide with surprise. "Is this what happened yesterday?"

"More or less," Rider growled, his hand going to his dagger.

Shit. I didn't want to get stabbed again. My arm still hurt and even though I was in my spirit form where physical pain was usually lessened, I couldn't afford anymore injuries, since injuries taken in our spirit form appeared on our bodies.

He's fine... more or less. Durand didn't drown him. He'll be okay. I mentally heaved at my shadow as Quill pressed a hand to my back and rubbed slow, calming circles.

But my shadow was furious that Sawyer had been in danger. He was mine, and I had to protect him. Mine!

No. Fuck! I thought at it. *Not mine.*

But my shadow didn't care. Sawyer had what it needed, was a perfect match for whatever that was, and it wasn't going to give him up. Ever. It would fight everyone and everything to keep its food source safe—

My thoughts stuttered at that. Food source was wrong. Sawyer wasn't just a means for it to stay alive, he was home. It needed to keep its *home* safe.

Which didn't make any sense because I was currently its home, not Sawyer.

CHAPTER 32
Talon

"FUCK ME," Ash groaned, his breath picking up, his unscarred cheek flushing with desire from the shadow's allure while Quill moaned softly and leaned into me, his lips seeking mine.

"Get your shadow under control," Rider growled, his body tense, affected as well.

Movement over his shoulder caught my attention and the new arrival with the red hair who I'd seen with Rider the other night — and who everyone in the Garden was talking about — materialized on the grass by the pool across from the bench.

Rider's gaze jerked to her as if he was suddenly aware of her presence and so did Ash's.

Was she the one they'd been looking for every time they glanced in that direction? Had Rider been expecting her to show up? And why the hell would

Rider be waiting for a woman? He didn't want a mate. Isemay's death had broken something inside him and he'd been adamant that he was never going to go through that again.

My shadow froze, its attention snapping to the redhead. She was... confusing. There was something about her that—

Realization swept through me. Except it wasn't my realization but my shadow's and I had no idea what it had figured out. It recognized something about the redhead and that filled me with a churning mix of confusing emotions I couldn't identify. Then it snapped back under my skin, curling into a tight ball in the heart of my magic and taking its allure with it. The others sagged with relief but I continued to spin, confused by its sudden withdrawal.

What the hell? I asked it.

But its response was more churning, confusing, hopeful, desperate, angry emotions that made no sense.

Ash shuddered and squeezed his eyes shut but couldn't seem to make himself turn away from the woman.

"Thanks a fucking lot," he ground out. "I still have four days before the novices can go to Lehyrst."

And because he was scarred, he thought no one in the Garden would be with him and he had to wait until Lehyrst.

“If you need—” I offered.

His discomfort was my fault. Ash wasn’t particularly interested in men and we’d never been intimate before, but sex was sex for me. With the exception of Quill — and Rider a long time ago — sex had been a means of survival for me and my shadow, nothing more.

“No. I can’t—” He bowed his head and squeezed his eyes tighter as if he was tempted to open them and continue staring at the woman.

He was the most magically sensitive of our group and could probably sense the power in the redhead’s marks. Even now their glow was strong enough for me to see from across the garden. With the way he magically connected with women, seeing that power and thinking she’d reject him had to be painful… probably as painful as my shadow’s desire for Sawyer.

“We need to figure out what’s going on with your shadow,” Quill said, his voice soft, his body still pressed against mine. “Just hearing about Sawyer in danger set it off. It’s never done that before.”

“We can’t afford to have you leave,” I replied.

And not just because I wanted him near, but because it looked like there was going to be trouble with this year’s group of novices and Quill was the best one to help Sawyer since I couldn’t trust myself to be anywhere near him.

"We can't afford to have it burst free again while you're at the Tower," he insisted.

"I can keep Sawyer safe," Ash ground out as he started to turn into smoke.

"Hold up." Rider sucked in a ragged breath, his attention still on the redhead. "It might not be your shadow that's the problem but the boy."

Ash resolidified but didn't look up at Rider, just kept his head down, not seeing that the redhead rose, glanced around then ran down the path away from the courtyard. Which was really strange since women who'd yet to find their first mate usually headed straight for the courtyard.

"Talon's shadow attacked the boy in a way we've never seen before, and now a shadow dragon just so happened to be flying near the Tower during the day," Rider said. "What if it's the boy, not your shadow? You said he's twice fae-touched."

"You think he has a magic that somehow attracts shadows?" Quill asked.

"Well, that would suck," Ash said through gritted teeth. "But come on. There's never been anything like that before, and the shadows are already acting strange. The boy wasn't around when a pair of big cats attacked Frost's team, and there have been more shadows out during the day."

"We can't risk it," Rider said. "Until we know what's

going on, Sawyer can't be beyond the Tower's barriers without at least a full Guardsman present."

"Then we're going to need to cut climbing holds in the ravine's edge." Ash's eyes flickered open then squeezed shut again and the muscles in his jaw flexed. "I doubt Mikel and his friends are going to stop ambushing Sawyer at the log bridge anytime soon, and the rest of the Guard will be pissed if you assign someone to watch the boy when he's running the trail."

Which was the biggest problem with Sawyer. He hadn't earned the Guardsmen's trust, and I hadn't done him any favors by attacking him yesterday and making him miss training. And as much as I usually agreed with Rider's philosophy of letting the men work it out among themselves, my shadow was pissed that Sawyer's life had been in danger and that he'd been hurt, not to mention been forced to run the trail while injured.

"And speaking of watching. I've really got to go." Ash vanished into a puff of smoke before we could confirm that we were meeting again tomorrow night.

A few yards away, two men materialized near another group of stone benches — since it was considered rude to materialize anywhere other than the lawn. They stepped onto the closest path heading to the courtyard, their attention locked on Rider, their expression a mix of fear and that same "lucky bastard" expression the other men had had.

"What the fuck is wrong with everyone?" he snarled. "I've been getting weird looks all night."

Quill shot me a questioning look, but I shrugged. I had no idea what was going on, either.

"I should go, too, and check the history books in the Black Tower's library tonight," Quill said. "I doubt I'll find anything, but it's worth a check. Tomorrow, I'll go to the White Tower and see if Briar has any new research on shadows."

"Also see if you can find out if there are any types of magic other than Talon's that might attract shadows," Rider added.

Quill nodded then vanished in a puff of smoke and Rider leveled his hard, silvery glare on me.

"Do you need to feed your shadow?" he asked, his wolf darkening his voice, and I couldn't tell if he was going to order me to find someone to fuck, or attack me and fuck me himself.

The thought sent a shiver rushing through me. I loved Quill, loved how we fit so perfectly together, but every now and then I missed Rider.

In the early days when I'd first been infected, Rider's ferocious, violent passions, had helped fuck my shadow into submission. But then he'd met Isemay and his love for her had shattered him.

And there wasn't anything I could do about it. He'd sworn he hadn't bonded with her, couldn't because she was human, but the way he reacted to her death told a different story, and most fae men never recovered from a broken soul bond with their female mate.

"It's not hungry," I said, making Rider raise his eyebrows in disbelief. "It's not. It's…" I had no idea what was wrong with it. "Sawyer has a lot of whatever it needs and its concerned about the boy being in danger."

"It needs to get over itself," Rider commanded. "The boy is a Guardsman. He's always going to be in danger."

But that only made my shadow more determined to protect him… which was going to be a serious problem when I had to leave the Gray and resume my post as Captain of the Gold Tower.

CHAPTER 33
Sage

I WOKE the next day sore and tired and afraid Rider was going to find out I hadn't actually gone to the infirmary. I prayed he'd think because I'd returned to training that the gash in my shin hadn't been too bad and wouldn't follow up with the healer over a lowly novice.

The injury had been deeper than I'd hoped, but I'd cleaned it up as best I could and wrapped it with lots of dressing — made from the shirt I'd worn to the Gray that I no longer needed — and pushed through the pain.

Thankfully, he didn't say anything about it at training that day and didn't bring up the shadow dragon attack. In fact, he was more gruff with me than before, which stung, given the moment I thought we'd shared after the attack and the fact that I knew deep down, he could be kind.

Adding to my mix of frustrating emotions was Talon, who continued to ignore me and kept his distance and Quill, who was missing.

Somehow, I managed to get through the day without needing to fight Talon's magic and without further injury.

Mikel and his friends didn't ambush me at the log bridge, but Durand looked like he really wanted to, so I set my horrible training plan in motion, letting it slip to Tyon that if he got friendlier with Talon or Lord Quill, Rider would go easier on him. I also mentioned that even though it didn't look like Rider was going easier on me, we all knew he'd be pissed if I ended up in the infirmary.

The next four days were an exercise in pain, exhaustion, and loneliness. My "training plan" worked and I got chased and tackled and dunked in the stream, earning me more bruises and scrapes and sore muscles but was never seriously injured — thank the Great father! And while it didn't feel as if I was getting better at anything, I knew if I just kept it up, I'd get faster at evading attacks and learn to recover faster after being struck or tackled.

Rider was even gruffer during regular training where I was sure the men were striking me harder than necessary, but still stopping before I ended up in the infirmary. Quill returned after two days away, stealing my breath all over again with his beauty, while Talon continued to ignore me and I *tried* to ignore him, except it was getting harder and harder not to glance at him.

Kit, Payne, and Lewin were still on the night shift, so mealtimes continued to be lonely with no relief from the sullen looks and snide remarks, but the worst was the Garden.

Before, my aches and injuries in my spirit form had been ghosts of what they were in my real body, but now I hurt almost as much in the Garden as I did in the Gray and my yearning for Fantasy Man — and Talon and Quill and Rider for that matter — grew stronger and stronger every night.

I kept going to the nook to hide from the other men, hoping, praying Fantasy Man would come for me, but it seemed Fantasy Man had also decided our last time was it for us.

Except knowing we'd both come to the same conclusion didn't ease the heat, pressure, and light radiating from my marks or my growing need for a sexual release.

I woke in the Black Tower on the last day of my first rotation as a Guardsman and forced myself to get out of bed. Every muscle in my body screamed in complaint, and I had no idea if I was ever going to get used to the physical demands of being a Guardsman or if my body was just going to give out.

Four more rotations, maybe five to be on the safe side, to ensure Sawyer had gotten out of the Great Five Kingdoms and then I could tell the truth and beg Lord Rider for mercy.

Except that thought made my chest and throat tighten.

As much as I hurt — Great Father I hurt! — and as much as I was lonely and always a little afraid that I'd be discovered, I also felt stronger.

I could look a man in the eyes, I could question him — I could insult him in the case of Mikel and his friends — and my life was still my own. They could hurt me, but they didn't have a say on who I married or when I ate or where I slept. I didn't have to serve them, and I didn't have to fear that I'd have to please one of them in bed if I didn't want to.

And after today, I had a two-day reprieve from training. Two days of glorious lieu time where I could spend all day in bed if I wanted to — which I definitely did.

I just had to get through the day.

I splashed water on my face, checked to make sure the scraps of my old dress that were flattening my chest were secure then checked the gash on my shin. The wound had scabbed over and the bruise around it had turned an ugly dark purple, but it wasn't warm to the touch which meant it wasn't infected even from daily dunkings in the stream.

With a steadying breath and the words, just one more day, running through my mind, I squared my shoulders, raised my chin, and stepped out of my room ready to face whatever the Guardsmen of the Black Tower threw at me.

Thankfully it was more of the same and I made it through the morning meal, stable duty, and the midday meal without incident — and, of course, without an orange.

I arrived early at the large boulders marking the entrance to the running trail and stared across the rugged, gray landscape to the Shadow Gate, barely visible in the mist. I hadn't been close to it yet, but I knew from my vision of Sawyer's death that it was enormous, wide enough for half a dozen carriages to pass through side by side.

There were two other gates, a white gate that led to the fae realm and a golden gate that led to the human realm, but I'd yet to see them. Were they as large as the Shadow Gate and just blended in better with the mist or were they smaller or farther away? There was so much I didn't know about... well, about everything.

The pasture gate in the Tower's tall, thick wall swung open and Talon and Lord Quill strode out, stealing my breath like they always did whenever I saw them. Why did they have to be so beautiful?

I tried to drag my attention back to the Shadow Gate but was just too tired to force myself to look away from Talon and Lord Quill. I'd passed my limit days ago, and the only reason I was still working and training was sheer force of will mixed with the fear that if I didn't, everyone would find out I was a girl.

Impossible sunlight glinted from Lord Quill's mess of golden locks as if he could summon light or part the mists around him, which I knew was impossible because Fantasy Man had said Lord Quill didn't possess magic and given how Fantasy Man had been trying to get me to look at other fae for possible mates, he had no reason to lie to me about that.

Lord Quill said something to Talon who glanced up, capturing my gaze with his despite the distance between us. I could barely see his eyes, let alone their mesmerizing swirls of pink, purple, blue, and gold, but I was still trapped and falling. A hint of darkness curled over one of his cheeks, but he didn't seem to notice and neither did Lord Quill, making me wonder if I'd really seen his shadow or just imagined it.

"Always so early," Lord Quill said.

"Yep," I replied still staring at Talon, the warmth and need of his seductive magic fluttering low inside me.

He stared back as if he was just as mesmerized by me. "How are you feeling?" he asked, his voice low.

A quip about being ready to take my daily bath in

the stream reached the tip of my tongue, but instinct made me swallow it back.

I'd forgotten myself with Lord Rider when I'd had the crap scared out of me by the shadow dragon, and he'd been gruff and aloof ever since. Better to be aloof as well, especially with Lord Quill present. Opening up around him might make him think he could press me for details about my "sister," and as much as a part of me would love to be rescued by Lord Quill that just wasn't an option.

And after the truth came out, it would be even less of an option.

No man wanted a woman who could fight. Even fae men who seemed to treat their women better than human men wouldn't want a woman who could swing a sword as well or better than they could... not that I would ever be able to fight as well as a fae.

"I'm fine," I forced out instead.

Lord Quill's eyes narrowed, but before he could tell me I obviously wasn't fine, the pasture gate opened and Lord Rider, along with most of the other novices marched out.

I moved away from them, fighting the urge to look at my feet and shrink in on myself. Men didn't try to make themselves smaller like women did. I had to keep my head up, make eye contact with them, and just get through one more day. Besides, they were helping me and just that knowledge gave me a glimmer of joy. Mikel would be pissed to know he was inadvertently training me so I could survive a future attack.

"Look who's sucking up to the captains," Mikel hissed as he drew closer.

Durand barked a harsh laugh. "More like *sucking off* the captains."

My thoughts instantly leaped to Talon in the bathhouse, water dripping from his beautiful, large cock.

The seductive ache of his magic flared to life within me and for a second it felt as if the mating marks I had in my spirit form burned around my neck and down my chest just like they had the last time Fantasy Man and I had made love.

I fought to hide my reaction, but my cheeks still heated with desire and embarrassment and there wasn't a damned thing I could do about it.

The other men snickered and Durand's expression darkened.

"You know the drill," Lord Rider growled, his attention — along with Lord Quill's and Talon's — on the other novices, thankfully not noticing my embarrassment. "Once around the trail, last one runs again with the rocks."

The novices took off, the fae taking the lead like they always did.

"See you at the log bridge, runt," Bramwell said as he shouldered past me, sending me stumbling.

One more day. That's all I needed to survive. One more. Not even. I just needed to get through training then half a shift at the stables and I had two glorious days of nothing. But before that, came one more dunk in the stream and today I was going to make them work for it.

CHAPTER 34

Sage

I HEADED down the trail not nearly as fast as usual, my sore muscles complaining, but I still managed to pass Tyon and four other of the slowest novices.

Bramwell no longer stopped to fake-tie his boots to get behind me and they didn't even bother to hide what they were doing from the other novices. Everyone was in on teaching me, the haughty lord, a lesson, and those who weren't directly involved, turned a blind eye to it.

After running the trail for the last eight days, I was familiar with the hills and turns and where the ground was uneven and I could stub my toe, so I let my mind wander, trying to come up with a plan of attack.

Three of them, usually led by Durand, always met me on this side of the stream, while Mikel and another always waited on the other side just in case I managed to slip past them. Not that I'd ever managed that, but maybe today would be the day.

I huffed a laugh at that. With how sore and tired I was, today wouldn't be the day. Next rotation… if they were still playing this particular game.

Ahead the trees thinned, and I ran across the narrow ridge with the steep slopes on either side, grateful that Mikel and his friends had picked the stream as the place they stop me. Being tossed into the stream wasn't nearly as dangerous as sliding across all that sharp shale.

The trail plunged back into the trees, and I pressed forward, determined to get this last fight before my lieu days over with.

Except as I reached the bend in the path and broke into the clearing before the log bridge, Durand leaped out of the underbrush and shoved me.

I stumbled and Bramwell pounced, grabbed my arm, and wrenched it painfully behind my back.

Shit. Ambushing me was new.

"Disgusting fae-touched runt," Durand sneered. "If you like cock so much, I'll give you cock."

He grabbed my belt and my pulse exploded into a desperate pounding. He was going to— I couldn't let him—

I yanked my knees up and rammed my feet into his stomach, shoving him back as I heaved against Bramwell's grip. But the bigger man was stronger than me, and Durand lurched forward, his lips curled back in a wicked sneer.

The other guys started yelling, probably encouragement, but all I could hear was a roar of voices and a wild rushing in my head.

I couldn't let him undress me. He'd know, and I doubted he'd stop once he knew I was actually a girl. Hell, no one was stopping him and they all thought I was a boy.

Oh, Great Father. This was what Sawyer had warned me about.

I'd thought I'd be safe, thought once I was discovered I'd be handed over to the Lord Commander, but I didn't take into account being discovered away from anyone who could save me.

They were going to—

No way in hell.

I heaved and flailed and kicked. I wouldn't let them have me. Not here. Not now. Not ever.

I managed to get one arm free and my fist cracked against Durand's jaw. With a snarl, he punched me in the gut, stealing my breath, and undid my belt buckle. My sword and dagger dropped to the ground, and he kicked them aside and reached for the laces on my pants.

"Stop," I begged. "Please. Stop."

"You think you're so special? Think letting the fae

captains fuck you will get you special treatment?" he spat.

"I'm not— I don't—"

He started to unlace my pants. I kicked out, but Durand blocked my strike and Ambrose leaped forward.

I couldn't let anyone else get a hold of me. I had to escape, no matter what. Fists and feet weren't doing it. I needed a weapon.

Both Durand's sword and dagger were close, but he'd stop me before I could draw them. Bramwell, however had a sword and two daggers, one on either hip.

I flailed behind me, hit the small hilt on his left side, and yanked the blade free.

Ambrose's eyes flashed wide, seeing me draw the weapon before Durand did, and he seized my wrist before I could strike and slammed his fist into my face.

My head jerked to the side, stars flashing across my vision.

"What the—?" Durand asked as Ambrose grabbed the front of my jerkin and tossed me over the edge of the ravine.

I crashed into the water, the world lurching around me, panic stealing my breath and shaking my body. I had to get away. Now now now.

"What the fuck?" Durand yelled.

"You were supposed to scare him, not actually fuck him," Hamelin said.

Mikel glared down at me from the far side of the ravine. "One word about this and we'll fuck you while you sleep." He turned his attention to the others and jerked his chin. "Come on."

Durand, Bramwell, and Ambrose ran across the log bridge, managing to keep their balance and they raced out of sight as I hugged myself, my stomach threatening to expel my lunch.

Not even Edred or Pylos had attacked me in that way. What the hell had I been thinking? I was stupid, so stupid. They'd almost— and I'd encouraged it.

A sob bubbled in my throat and I clamped my hands over my mouth to stop it. I couldn't cry. I was a man. Men didn't cry.

Except I was scared. I'd only ever been more scared facing the shadow monsters, and — Great Father! — it hadn't been because being discovered would endanger Sawyer, it was because of what I knew they'd do to me once they learned the truth.

I lurched up stream away from the bridge and the other runners who'd come by, my stomach heaving, bile burning my throat, and my face throbbing from where Ambrose had hit me. Tears stung my eyes but somehow, I managed to hold it back until I was out of sight. Then I pressed my hands over my mouth to muffle my sobs and cried.

I cried for fear of what had almost happened and how I had to run back into the practice grounds and pretend nothing *had* happened because I couldn't go running to Lord Rider or Talon or Lord Quill for help. That would only prove to them that I was the spoiled nobleman letting the fae fuck him to get special treatment.

And then I cried for Sawyer and the life he should have had and for our mother and father and brother. I wanted to save him, to save all of them, and I was too weak. I'd failed the rest of our family. My premonitions had told me they were in danger and I'd still been helpless. What made me think I wouldn't fail Sawyer?

I was never going to beat Edred at his own game. I was just a girl. Weak and pathetic. What made me think I could fight? What made me think I could survive as a Guardsman for a rotation let alone four?

I couldn't. Durand and his friends had just proven I couldn't, and now it was clear they wouldn't stick to attacking me on the trail. Mikel had promised they'd attack me in the middle of the night while my soul was stuck in the Garden.

I wasn't safe here. I wasn't safe anywhere, not even in my home where I was supposed to be safe.

Something inside me snapped at that thought and a red-hot rage consumed my fear. How dare they take away what little safety I had in the Gray. I had been doing fine. Fine!

I marched through the water to the holes that had been cut in the ravine wall the day after the shadow dragon had attacked me and climbed out.

As ridiculous as it was, I had hoped that once I was discovered things would work out. It had been a small hope, and I hadn't fully realized I'd still had it, but I had, and now that was gone.

I marched back to the log bridge, crossed it to retrieve my sword belt then crossed it again and half jogged half stormed my way down the trail.

If all hope was lost, if keeping my head down — more or less — wasn't keeping me safe and I'd fucked it up by trying my stupid plan to become a better fighter, then it didn't matter what I did.

I wasn't ever going to be safe, my life was over, and Durand, Mikel, Ambrose, and the others were going to pay for that.

I crested the last hill on the trail. Lords Rider, Quill, and Talon stood by the sparring circles talking while the novices sat around, the fae looking bored while the less experienced humans all huffed, trying to catch their breaths.

"Glad you could finally join us, Sawyer." Rider glanced at me then turned back to his conversation with Quill and Talon.

Funnily, with my rage burning through me, it was easy to not fall into Talon or Quill's eyes and focus on the men who'd attacked me.

Durand sneered at me and Mikel looked smug, while Bramwell and Hamelin looked slightly concerned but not as upset as they should have given that they'd tried to rape me.

"Remember what I told you," Mikel hissed as I stalked up to them.

"And you remember this," I hissed back as I stopped beside Ambrose and glared at the others. "Try that again and I will slit your throats while you sleep."

"Don't make idle threats," Durand huffed. "They'd execute you for that."

"Look in my eyes and tell me my threat is idle," I snarled back, letting them see the fury boiling within me, my body trembling with rage.

Durand's eyes widened and Hamelin hissed an, "Oh, shit."

"Oh, and Ambrose," I said as I turned to him.

He raised his gaze to me and I rammed my fist as hard as I could into his face. His nose broke with a satisfying crunch, his expression complete shock at what had just happened.

In fact, everyone stared at me, the world stuttering to a stop, unable to believe what just happened.

Then everything lurched back into action and everyone reacted and gasped and yelled.

"Sawyer!" Lord Rider roared, silencing the chaos as quickly as it had erupted.

I turned to face him, his body tense and vibrating

with his fury, his feral, predatory nature burning through his silver gaze.

Everything within me screamed to make myself smaller, apologize, beg for his forgiveness, but I clamped down on that and raise my chin. I was angry and I had every right to be angry. I was *not* going to back down on this. I wouldn't tattle, but I also wouldn't let them think they could attack me like that again.

"Run the trail," he snarled.

"How many laps?" I asked, standing my ground.

"I said run! You run until I fucking tell you to stop." He lurched toward me, and I instinctively flinched back, the look of violence in his eyes too much like Edred's and Pylos's.

CHAPTER 35
Rider

FEAR SWEPT over the rage in Sawyer's eyes, and he bolted for the mouth of the running trail as my wolf strained to take control and chase after him. What the fuck had possessed the boy? He'd threatened the lives of his fellow novices and then broken Ambrose's nose. And while I was sure they deserved it, Sawyer had attacked a fellow Guardsman in front of me, which meant he was the one I had to punish.

"Enough," I snarled at the other novices. "You haven't put the boy in his place. All you've shown him is that he can't trust you. Right now, if you face a shadow with him, he's going to stand back and let it tear you to shreds—"

Mikel opened his mouth to say something, and I snapped my attention to him, my wolf curling my lips back and releasing a snarl, silencing whatever idiotic defense he was going to make.

"And I'd be standing right beside him watching. That isn't special treatment—"

My claws and canines extended, and I didn't bother to fight it. Let them see just how pissed off I was. It was about fucking time.

"That's survival. If he can't trust you, I can't trust you. If you want to compete for a place on an elite team, you better show me that your fellow Guardsmen trust you and you can follow fucking orders!"

I raked my glare over them, watching both the human and fae novices shrink back from my beast's fury.

Quill and Talon stepped up beside me, adding their glare to mine. Not that it was necessary or intimidating, but they were making it clear that on this, we, the leaders of the Black Guard, were a united front.

I was actually thoroughly impressed with Talon for not completely losing his shit. I had no doubt it was taking everything for him to hold his shadow at bay. Sawyer had looked furious and shocked and terrified and was sporting a new bright red bruise on his cheek. Whatever they'd done, it had crossed a line.

One more fuck up and I was done playing nice. I didn't care how much I needed Guardsmen or if I had to have proof. If I and the other Guardsmen couldn't trust these novices, they didn't belong in the Guard, and since I couldn't send the humans back, they were going to have the most menial service positions I could give them for the rest of their lives.

"I punished Sawyer for coming through the ring after dark, and you thought it wasn't enough. You think you know better?" I leveled my gaze on Mikel. "Then *you* should be Lord Commander. Come and take it from me."

Mikel glanced at Durand, then Bramwell, Hamelin, and Ambrose — whose hands were still clamped over his nose, blood oozing between his fingers.

"Don't look at them." I flexed my fingers, my claws getting even bigger, almost too big for my hands, and fur swept up over my forearms. "You took Sawyer's discipline into your own hands, so you must want to challenge me for leadership of the Guard."

"It wasn't— I didn't—" Mikel stammered.

"What about you?" I glared at Durand, who inched away, then at Hamelin and Bramwell, who hung their heads, scared and ashamed. "How about you?" I snarled, leveling my gaze on Ambrose.

"The Lord Commander asked you a question," Quill barked, making the novices jump. "Are you challenging him for leadership?"

"No, my lord," Ambrose gasped and Bramwell bobbed his head in agreement.

"I can't hear you." Quill set his hand on the hilt of his sword.

"No, my lord," they all called back, louder this time, their voices edged with fear.

"Good," Quill said. "The men are yours, Lord Commander."

My wolf huffed at him. It wanted to hunt, to tear something to pieces, and was pissed that no one had accepted my challenge.

"Ambrose," I snarled, my wolf darkening my voice, making the man's breath pick up and his eyes widen with fear. "Go to the infirmary and get that fixed. Everyone else, grab a practice sword, pair up, and start sparring."

The men all scrambled to obey me as I watched, seething that it had come to this.

I let Talon and Quill handle the afternoon's sparring, watching from the corner of my eye as Sawyer came down the final hill on the trail and went back up the first, going around and around, his laps getting slower and slower. I wanted to calm down before dealing with the boy, but every time I saw him stagger down that hill, I heard his threat.

I will slit your throats while you sleep.

Sawyer wasn't the risk for suicide that Ash and Talon had first thought. He was at risk for murder.

The boy who understood Talon's condition, who Kit had said was smart and thoughtful and had come through the ring after dark because he'd been getting his sister to safety, had been pushed to the very edge and was about to snap.

And that continued to inflame my wolf's rage. Ash had said he'd taken whatever Mikel and friends had thrown at him without complaint for the last few days — he even seemed to be using it to better his reflexes and learn to anticipate attacks. He wouldn't have just snapped over that or over the blow to his face. It had to have been—

The boy stumbled down the last hill, lost his balance and skidded the last few feet on his knees, ripping his pants.

Damn it. I should have stopped him sooner. He shouldn't have done the last couple—

Fuck, how many laps had he done?

The seventh bell rang, ending the afternoon's training session, and my stomach bottomed out. I'd made him run for the entire session. Even if it had been at the beginning of a rotation that would have been too much for a novice, and Sawyer had been working hard for days. It was actually a miracle he'd run for as long as he had.

With a groan, he shoved himself to his feet and staggered toward the trail's first hill... because I hadn't told him to stop yet and when I'd yelled at him he'd had that same look in his eyes when we'd first squared off in the sparring ring, the one that told me he'd been beaten frequently by someone before he'd come to the Tower.

"Enough," I barked, striding toward him, unable to keep my and my wolf's anger from my tone.

Goddess I was so angry. Angry that Sawyer was about to snap, angry that the humans would send me a child, angry that other humans couldn't behave themselves, and angry at letting my anger overwhelm me enough to lose track of how many laps Sawyer had run.

He stumbled to a stop then valiantly, foolishly, fought to keep standing before collapsing to his hands and knees, gasping for breath. With a groan, his back heaved, and he threw up, not even trying to avoid his hands let alone get off the trail.

I was a monster. I should have paid more attention — hell, I shouldn't have punished him in the first place because it was obvious he'd been defending himself. But there were some lines that couldn't be crossed and attacking a fellow Guardsman in front of the Lord Commander or the captains outside of a sparring ring was one of them.

"You never attack another Guardsman," I snarled. I never wanted to make him run like that again.

His back heaved again and he gasped something that might have been the start of an acknowledgement but ended in him puking again.

"You're relieved from stable duty this evening."

Because I doubted he'd be able to stand, let alone handle all but the most placid nags we used for supply runs.

Talon and Quill watched with wary eyes, knowing one small thing could set off my wolf.

"And you're restricted to the Tower for your lieu days. I expect to see better self control when the new rotation starts." I forced myself to turn away, fighting the urge to tell him a part of me was actually proud of him for standing up to the others. I couldn't condone what he'd done or show him mercy. That would only make the matter worse.

Talon opened his mouth to say something and took a hesitant step toward Sawyer, but my wolf snarled at him. "You have to leave him."

"I hate this," he murmured back, his body tense and half of his skin black with his shadow.

"So do I," I huffed, "but he broke Ambrose's nose in front of everyone."

"Knowing Sawyer, the man probably deserved it," Quill said, grabbing Talon's hand and tugging him after me.

Talon pulled out of Quill's grasp but didn't turn back to help the boy. "I wonder which one of those assholes is Ash."

"Best guess, Hamelin or Bramwell," I said, yanking open the pasture gate and storming inside the Tower's bailey.

“I really hope it’s Ambrose,” Talon huffed. “Would serve him right for letting it go as far as it did. Did you see how scared he was?”

“Did you see how angry?” Quill added. “He was already hesitant with… well, with everyone. It’s going to be that much harder to earn his trust now.”

“I know.” I ran my hands through my hair, pulling out my topknot and not giving a fuck that I didn’t look like the in-control-lord-commander I was supposed to be. “But he trusts Kit, Payne, and Lewin. We should build on that.”

“How are we going to do that without it looking like one of us is giving him special treatment?” Quill asked.

“I don’t know,” I snarled.

“We could move the advanced novices’ rotation to the second shift, then at least his mealtime would line up with theirs,” Talon suggested.

“Except the other Guardsmen would know we were making a concession for him because novice training is always the first shift,” Quill said.

“At the very least, find Kit and tell him the boy is stuck in the Tower for the next two days and isn’t restricted to a specific mealtime,” I said, reaching a door near the great hall and yanking it open. “He can at least eat with them during his lieu time.”

“If he’s up to getting down to the great hall,” Talon replied, reminding me that *I* was the reason he was probably still on his hands and knees on the running trail dry heaving.

Fuck!

My wolf's ferocious nature flared, and I seized the front of Talon's jerkin and shoved him into the wall with more force than I wanted.

"Tell them to bring the boy food or carry him down, or whatever," I growled in his face. "I don't care what, but we can't completely lose his trust."

I didn't know why it was suddenly so important, but the thought of him hating me or despising his life here in the Tower squeezed my chest so tight I could barely breathe and made my bones ache with my wolf's need to shift.

He was a promising fighter. Even if he never had a growth spurt and stayed his pathetically small size, he was already close to being as good as a regular Guardsman with the potential of becoming great.

CHAPTER 36
Rider

I LEFT Quill and Talon to find my cousin and his mate and stomped to the kitchen to grab my dinner then stomped up to my room. I really needed to let my wolf out and go hunting but I couldn't afford missing my meeting with Ash in the Garden. I had to know what the fuck happened on the trail. And fuck— It was the last day of the rotation.

The four of us were to meet Lark and her mates and celebrate the new novices.

We'd started the ritual a couple of decades ago after I'd become the Lord Commander and Talon, Quill, and Ash had become captains. The demands of our new jobs had kept us too busy for our usual family gatherings and the pressures of the job had made it more difficult for me to control my primal nature.

Lark had gotten frustrated and worried and

insisted on a number of gatherings that happened every year, in part to see me and the other guys — who'd she'd become friends with when we'd all been grunts in the Black Guard — and in part to use her magic to communicate with animals to help calm my beast.

Which was something I really needed right now.

As much as my wolf wanted to skip whatever Lark had planned for this evening and go hunting, my human half knew spending time with Lark would actually be better. She always helped me regain control and she usually inadvertently ended up helping Talon and Quill, too.

Time inched by as I picked at my dinner, unable to find my appetite. Then I paced my small sitting room waiting for when I had to manifest to the Garden.

I could go early, but then I'd just be pacing in the Garden and the urge to shift and hunt would be stronger — since shifting while in my spirit form didn't hurt nearly as much as it did when I was in my body.

That and the lure of the forest bordering the Garden would call to me. It was filled with small game just for beast-fae like me since hunting sometimes helped satisfy some of our beast's ferocity before having sex with our mate. And even if the small game wasn't as exciting to my wolf as shadows, it was still hunting.

Finally, the water clock I'd started at the eighth bell

indicated it was time and I threw myself onto my bed, closed my eyes, and manifested in the Garden by the benches where we'd agreed to meet.

And of course, I fucking appeared facing the pool where Sage always manifested. My attention instantly swept over the area, searching for her like it had every night since I'd seen her, and my heart stuttered with the disappointment that she wasn't there.

Which, on top of everything that was going on, was just fucking great.

Even with the shit from the novices and the increased number of shadows and the Guard's decreased ranks, I still — fucking still! — looked for her. And that made me feel as if I was dishonoring Isemay's memory.

In a few days, I'd mark yet another year without her, another year where I had to live with the choices that had killed her, and even though fae couldn't bond with humans the way we bonded with other fae, I still felt as if her death had ripped a hole in my heart and soul.

She was my mate. There'd been no one else and there'd never be anyone else.

So why the hell couldn't I stop looking for and thinking of Sage?

And really! I should be thinking about Sawyer and my fucking novices, not some woman.

"Waiting for a certain redhead?" Wells asked from behind me.

My wolf tensed, and I wrenched my attention from the pool to the fae standing at the mouth of a path that disappeared around a large tree and headed into the forested area. He must have just come around the corner and seen me because he sure as hell hadn't been there before... of course I hadn't really been looking for anyone. I'd been instantly drawn to where Sage should have been—

Fuck, no. *Could* have been. She *shouldn't* have been anywhere.

"Fascinating, isn't she?" Wells took a step closer, and my wolf snarled, stopping him in his tracks. "So, the rumors about you are true."

"What rumors?" And why the hell would there be any rumors about me? No one had paid attention to me in the Garden since I'd yelled at Ember in no uncertain terms that I was never going to be her mate.

Except people *had* been paying attention to me lately. I'd been getting strange looks for days. Ember had even walked by, staring daggers at me as if I'd offended her when it had been years since I'd rejected her.

"You know," Wells purred. "The ones about you deciding it was time to be mated. The ones about you courting a certain redhaired new arrival."

"Sage?"

"Ah, so that's her name." Wells's lips curled into a wicked smile.

Everyone thought I was courting Sage? That was ridiculous.

"I've talked to her once." All right, it wasn't technically once, but the first time... or was that the second time didn't count. One of the times hadn't counted... not really... because I didn't want a mate.

"I've heard it's more than just once." Wells shrugged. "I heard from a little redhaired birdie that you've made your intentions clear and it's official."

She told him that? How could she? I helped her get her bearings in the Garden and — all right fine! — I talked to her twice, but I sure as hell didn't tell her I was courting her.

Goddess be damned! I had more than enough to deal with than a woman trying to snag me by spreading lies.

"We're not courting," I snarled.

Ember had tried something similar and I'd been forced to make her rejection public.

What the fuck was wrong with these new arrivals that they thought *I* would make a good mate? I'd make a horrible mate. Even if I wasn't a barely contained animal who commanded the Black Guard I was still in love with Isemay.

"You're not?" Wells pressed.

"Of course not. I've never courted a woman and I

never will," I insisted as the swirling smoke of Talon, Quill, and Ash blossomed to life beside me. "Now fuck off. I've got business."

"Of course, Lord Commander," Wells drawled, his tone mocking.

With another lazy shrug, he turned and strode back down the path, and I tried to rein in my wolf's rage that Sage would spread lies about me courting her.

The smoke of my friends' manifesting spirit forms swirled together, entwining for a moment, each of them vying for the spot they'd all been aiming for before separating and solidifying into the men — because the Garden wouldn't let spirits manifest in the same place at the same time.

"What happened?" Talon demanded, turning on Ash the moment he'd fully formed. His shadow writhed around his body, the control he'd had during training completely gone, and a wave of seductive heat and need from his allure slammed into me.

I suddenly needed to be at Sage's pool to greet her, to be with her. But she'd lied and I didn't want a mate. I had more important things to worry about, damn it.

Ash groaned and dropped onto the bench beside him, his gaze jerking to Sage's pool. "Get a hold of yourself."

"He's mine," Talon— no, his shadow snarled, shocking the hell out of me. Before running across

Sawyer the other day, I'd never seen or heard his shadow control him like that. "Mine! And he was terrified. You were supposed to protect him."

"I did." Ash squeezed his eyes shut but couldn't seem to turn his head.

Was he mesmerized by Sage like I was? Maybe it had something to do with her magic. That would explain why I kept thinking of her when Isemay was my one and only mate.

Except that made me think of mating and instead of imagining Isemay's warm smile, I saw Sage's stunned, green eyes staring at me.

"I did protect him," Ash gasped. "The boy pulled a dagger and I got him out of the situation before they killed him."

"But you let it get far enough that he drew his blade." Talon's shadow jerked him forward and he raised his fist to punch Ash, but Quill grabbed his arm and wrenched him back.

"This won't help him, Talon," he said, his voice low and soothing. "Pull it back so Ash can talk."

Talon's shadow huffed, but the surge of need that was on its way to making my cock rock hard and flooding me with images of red hair and green eyes eased, and the shadow sank back under his skin.

"Talk," Talon's shadow hissed.

"In short, they think the boy is letting you fuck him

for special favors, and Durand, in particular, wanted to take his share," Ash said.

Talon's shadow erupted from his body again and jerked him to his feet, his hands clenched and his eyes filled with rage, as my wolf snarled and heaved against my control as well. Now it didn't just want to rip something apart, it wanted to rip Durand apart. No one treated a fae-touched like that in the Guard. No one!

"He didn't do it. I broke it up before it happened," Ash said in a hurry, then he barked a half laugh. "That boy has a spark that just won't die. I knew he'd be upset, but I didn't expect him to come off the trail and threaten to murder us. And did you see that punch on Ambrose? Holy fuck it was beautiful."

"I had to punish him for that," I growled, hating myself even more now that I knew what the novices had done.

"But it was a thing of beauty. Completely unexpected, decisive, hard. Sawyer's been duck and scramble with quick, weak attacks because he knows if anyone gets their hands on him, he's done," Ash said, finally managing to yank his attention away from Sage's pool and lock gazes with me. "But that punch—"

"Was reckless," I said, cutting him off. "If it had been any other situation, Ambrose would have attacked back."

"But it wasn't about attacking and you know that,"

Ash pressed. “It was about sending a message and with your little speech afterward, not to mention the conversations that I overheard once training was over, it looks like the men received that message loud and clear.”

“You think they’ll leave Sawyer alone?” Talon asked.

“To the point of isolating him,” Ash replied, his expression grim. “But I think the attacks on the trail are over.”

I could only hope Ash was right. I didn’t want to have to punish Sawyer again, and I didn’t want him to feel that murder was his only option for staying safe.

CHAPTER 37

Sage

I WASN'T sure how long I sat on the running path, trembling with fatigue and pain and frustration and anger, although it couldn't have been that long since I didn't hear the eighth bell call the second shift to dinner.

A few guardsmen who were still in the sparring yard glanced my way, but no one offered to help — not that I expected anyone to. No, if I'd had any doubts about everyone in the Black Tower despising me, they'd vanished as I wiped the puke off my hands onto the thighs of my ripped pants, staggered to my feet, and hobbled back to the Tower.

I didn't bother with dinner. I wouldn't have been able to keep hold of my anger at the comments, looks, and attempts to trip me. The fear I'd felt when Rider had yelled at me had burned away after the tenth time around the track and he still hadn't told me to stop.

I didn't care that I knew a softer, kinder Rider in the Garden. That Rider had to be a lie, a mask he wore when he was with a woman. If that had been the real Rider, he wouldn't have made me run until I threw up.

And then Talon and Quill had shown their true colors as well, turning their backs on me and walking away even though I was clearly unwell.

A part of me knew they couldn't have helped me without proving Mikel and the others right. Helping me after I threatened to kill them and then broke Ambrose's nose would definitely be special treatment. But Durand trying to rape me only proved I'd never make friends with any of them anyway, so it didn't matter if I got special treatment or if they thought I was spoiled and arrogant or not.

They weren't going to change their minds about me, and I was done trying to win them over or even just go unnoticed. I just needed to get through four, maybe five more rotations to ensure Sawyer's safety, and then I could turn myself over to Rider.

That thought flickered icy fear within me that made me want to scream, but I swallowed it back as I struggled up the three flights of stairs to my floor in the barracks.

After this afternoon, I couldn't trust Rider to protect me when I revealed the truth. He might be kind to fae women, but that didn't mean he'd be kind to a human woman.

At best, he'd return me to Edred. At worst, he'd punish me before sending me back... or never send me back. He'd been furious when I'd threatened the others, and I doubted he'd just wanted to send me running around the trail.

He wasn't able to take his anger out on another Guardsman, but once I revealed I was a woman, there'd be nothing to stop him from letting loose.

Edred had looked at me and Sawyer the same way Rider had when I'd broken Ambrose's nose, and I had no doubt if Edred hadn't arranged a good bride price for me or had figured out a way for no one to notice I was gone, he'd have locked me in Herstind Castle's dungeon and punched and whipped and cut his frustration into my body until I died.

But there was no escape from Rider. I was magically bound to the Black Tower so I couldn't just run away. All I could do was hope I could keep my identity a secret long enough for Sawyer to get out of the Five Great Kingdoms.

Except how could I manage that when everyone was watching me?

I bit back another scream and opened the door at the top of the stairs. The barracks' hallway with the dozens of plain wooden doors on either side had never looked so long before.

I shouldn't have encouraged the rumor that I was getting special treatment, and I certainly shouldn't have used their bullying to try to become a better fighter.

Shadows above, I still had my impending death to deal with.

I still didn't know when I'd be attacked, but given how things had soured so quickly with the other novices and the fact that they thought I was Sawyer in my vision, it had to happen soon. No matter what I wanted, if Mikel and Durand and their self-made elite team of human fighters were going to retaliate for my threats, they'd do it soon. And I wasn't anywhere near ready to face them.

This afternoon had more than proven that.

Sure, I'd managed to draw Bramwell's dagger, but Ambrose had disarmed me before I'd even realized what he was doing.

I could try keeping pace with some of the other novices not involved in the group, but I doubted that would help.

Like all the other times, they'd just pretend they didn't notice and keep on running the trail, probably happy that they weren't going to be the ones running with the bag of rocks after the training session.

I finally reached the end of the hall and staggered into my room. My legs were so sore and weak, I could barely stand, but I managed to lean against my wash basin and wash my hands and rinse out my mouth before collapsing on my bed. My clothes were sweaty and grimy, and I'd ripped both pantlegs and skinned my knees, but I didn't have the energy to do more. And Great Father help me if I ended up in the Garden—

A whisper of a warm breeze tickled my cheek, carrying with it the soft, sweet scent of the flowers in the Garden.

Stupid— Fucking— Not now!

I squeezed my eyes tighter and tried to will myself back into my body in the Black Tower, but it was like the scent of those softly glowing pink and white flowers had gotten stuck in my nose and kept growing stronger. Then the far-off sound of masculine voices and laughter joined in and I knew I was stuck.

Come on!

I didn't want to have to deal with avoiding the men in the Garden, and I particularly didn't want to risk running into Rider. I wouldn't be able to pretend he hadn't made me run until I'd dropped and I'd end up yelling at him. With my luck, he'd probably figure out everything and that would be the end of that.

Which meant if I wanted to avoid him and everyone else, I needed to get out of the open. Anyone could see me right now with a simple glimpse from the courtyard onto the manicured lawns of the garden.

CHAPTER 38

Sage

I FORCED myself to sit up, every muscle aching as much as when I'd collapsed on my bed. Even my cheek still stung, and I suspected if I looked in a mirror, the bruise Ambrose had given me would be fresh and red even though I was in my spirit form.

I didn't know why I felt all my pain and exhaustion now when I hadn't before. Perhaps I'd finally reached my limit, and the strain of the rotation had sunk in deep enough to affect my spirit. I could only hope that meant I wouldn't be here long and would actually get a full night's sleep.

Thankfully, no one waited for me on the bench on the grass across the shallow pool and there was no one on the lawn or the paths nearby.

With a groan, I stood and, half walking half staggering, hobbled away from the courtyard before someone noticed me.

I didn't want to spend any more time than necessary wandering the Garden, so I headed straight to the nook. Fantasy Man hadn't shown up for days, and even if he did, I wouldn't have said no to some gentle, relaxed sex.

Although he'd probably take one look at me and know how sore and tired and angry and — if I was being honest with myself — how scared I was and just offer to hold me.

Which I wouldn't say no to, either.

The idea of his strong arms around me and the sense of safety I always felt when I was with him tightened my throat.

I'd been trying to be strong for days— years if I counted the time after my mother died and Edred took control of my life. Add on the stress of hiding my identity from everyone in the Black Tower, the physical rigors of Guardsman training, and the attacks from the other Guardsmen and I knew it was just a matter of time before I broke.

Perhaps letting go and crying in Fantasy Man's arms would help. At least here I was a woman and didn't have to be strong all the time. With luck, Fantasy Man wouldn't ask for details and I wouldn't have to come up with a lie.

Sure, we had a relationship, but it wasn't a close

one. We hadn't even told each other our names and I didn't know what he looked like. We had sex and we flirted. That was all.

My throat tightened and tears burned my eyes at that thought.

Which was ridiculous. I didn't know him so I couldn't possibly care for him. I was just lonely and afraid, and he was the only one in my new crazy life who I felt I could trust.

Of course, maybe he was just using me or lying and manipulating me and would turn on me the minute he thought he'd won my trust.

And now I was letting my fear and exhaustion twist my thoughts. He might be lying to me, but I was definitely lying to him and using him for sex and comfort as well.

Just like the previous nights, Fantasy Man wasn't waiting for me in the grove. My throat tightened even more and my eyes burned with tears that I knew were irrational.

I hadn't expected him to be there so I shouldn't have been so disappointed.

With a pathetic half moan half sob, I sagged onto the bench, eased my aching body against the sloping arm facing the entrance, and closed my eyes.

Four more rotations. Four more rotations.

That was all I had to last.

Something crunched by the entrance and my pulse fluttered with hope.

Fantasy Man had come.

Except when I sat up and looked, it wasn't my Fantasy Man. It was Wells and Crane and my flutter of hope turned into gut-twisting worry.

"You shouldn't be here," I said. "Rider will be here in a moment."

It had been a few days since I'd lied and said Rider was courting me, and I hadn't thought Wells and Crane were dumb or forgetful, but maybe I'd been mistaken.

Wells's lips curled back in a predatory smile that turn the gut-twisting worry in my stomach to ice and made my pulse pick up.

"Rider isn't coming," he purred, his hungry eyes sliding over my body and making me feel naked even though I was fully dressed.

"Of course he is," I insisted, fighting the urge to cover myself with my arms. I couldn't show any fear — or any more fear than I already was. That would only satisfy a man like Wells and I didn't want him satisfied. I wanted him to go away.

"We know he's not," Crane shot back, taking a step closer. "We've been watching you for days now. You always come here and no one else joins you."

"Oh, and I talked with Rider." Wells's grin turned smug as he sauntered to the silver fence separating the nook from the bedroom where I'd watched Lark and her mates make love.

He trailed his fingers over the vines wrapped around the metal, brushing the pink and white flowers and making their light tremble. "He seemed pretty upset that you lied about him courting you."

Of course he was, because he wasn't the man he pretended to be when he was in the Garden.

That thought reignited my anger at him and Talon and Quill… and myself.

I was stupid for thinking I could trust them, for believing I'd be safe with them either here or in the Gray, and now Wells and Crane were leering at me, thinking because Rider didn't have a claim to me — as if I was still property even though they all thought I was fae — that I was now theirs.

Rider had said I should put these boys in their place and Ember, the fae woman who'd commanded the entire courtyard like a goddess, wouldn't have stood for Wells and Crane looking at her like she was their next meal.

That, and I was sore and tired and wanted to break Ambrose's nose again for making me feel like this. Once hadn't been nearly enough.

"Go away," I said, giving my first ever order to a man, my stomach bottoming out with my boldness. "I'm not interested."

The urge to flee twisted inside me and I stood.

Except to leave, I had to pass Crane, and Mikel and his friends had already proven I didn't stand a chance against a human, let alone a larger fae.

"We don't care if you're interested," Wells said. "You're going to be our mate."

"It doesn't work that way," I said, straightening and trying to look commanding like Ember had. *Focus on your anger not your fear.*

But Crane leaped forward, the movement sudden and quick, and my fear spiked.

I jerked back, narrowly avoiding his hands, the *lessons* Mikel and the others had taught me actually coming in handy. But I couldn't keep my balance with my weakened muscles. My heel caught on the foot of the bench and I toppled backward.

Crane grabbed my arm before I could fall and wrenched me forward. He captured me with one hand pressing me against his chest and the other holding my arm up.

Wells snapped an intricately wrought silver bracelet around my wrist, and white-hot agony exploded inside me. It shot out from my heart to the tips of my fingers and toes and over my scalp in a quick violent burst before extinguishing, leaving me shuddering and gasping.

"What did you do?"

"Ensured that you can't send your spirit back to your body," Wells said.

“What?” I heaved against Crane’s grip, but an exhaustion greater than I’d ever experience before swelled over me and I sagged against him.

“You’re here until we complete the spell that will initiate the mating bonds with us,” he said as he scooped me up into his arms, the exhaustion stuttering for a moment before overwhelming me again.

“You’re making me tired,” I said, my words slurred.

“Yes,” Crane said as a terrible hunger filled his yellow eyes. “And I’m going to make you feel a lot more once you’re our mate.”

Don't miss the next book in the series!

Whispers Within the Midnight Garden

Desperate Disguise: Book Three

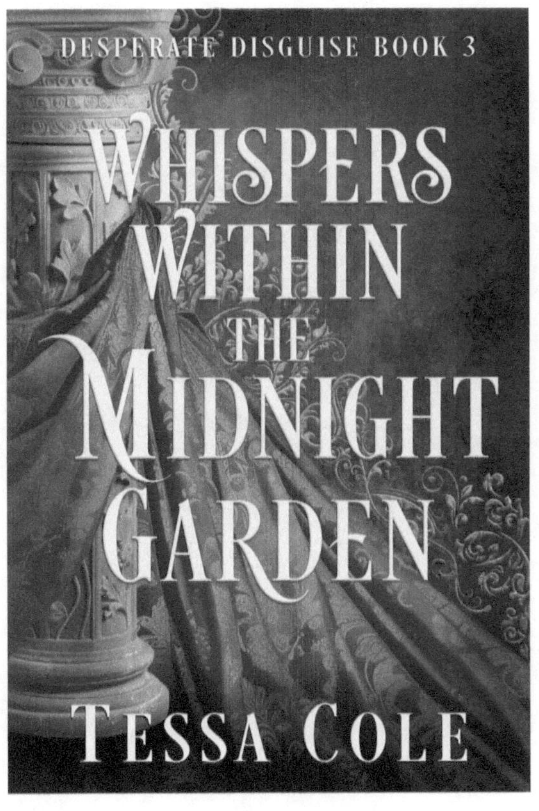

Other Books by Tessa Cole

DESPERATE DISGUISE

Lies Within the Darkest Tower, book 1

Stand Against the Rising Storm, book 2

Whispers Within the Midnight Garden, book 3

NEPHILIM'S DESTINY

Destined Shadows, prequel story

Destined Darkness, book 1

Destined Blood, book 2

Destined Fire, book 3

Destined Storm, book 4

Destined Radiance, book 5

ANGEL'S FATE

Fated Bonds, book 1

Fated Winter, book 2

Fated Fear, book 3

Fated Despair, book 4

Fated Resolve, book 5

Fated Heart, book 6

ENSNARED BY THE PACK

Wolf Deceived, book 1

Wolf Denied, book 2

Wolf Desired, book 3

Wolf Distressed, book 4

Wolf Decided, book 5

Wolf Devoted, book 6

THE GRECIAN GODDESS TRILOGY

Written with Clara Wils

Kiss of the Goddess, book 1

Power of the Goddess, book 2

Bonds of the Goddess, book 3

SECRETS GODS KEEP

Written with Clara Wils

Craving Demons, book 1

Chaos Demons, book 2

Claiming Demons, book 3

HER BAD BOY WOLVES

Written with Clara Wils

Pack Against the Wall, book 1

Want you Pack, book 2

Pack in Business, book 3

www.ingramcontent.com/pod-product-compliance
Lightning Source LLC
Chambersburg PA
CBHW031542240626
47153CB00002B/351

* 9 7 8 1 9 9 0 5 8 7 6 3 4 *